Dakota Manhunt

Clint McCorg had been elected Sheriff of Vendado – with orders to uphold law and order in a town fast heading for an era of lawlessness worse than anything it had experienced in its short history.

Being forced to kill a man two years earlier had turned McCorg into a hard, bitter man with the kind of reputation that made men think twice before moving their hands towards their holstered guns. He had been sheriff for less than six months when trouble flared in town and three innocent men were kidnapped from one of the hotels and taken out of Vendado. Their bodies were found the next day, hands lashed behind their backs and bullets in their bodies.

Now it was McCorg's job to go out after the killers – men who scorned the reputation of this hardened lawman. He knew that he was up against big trouble, but even so, he had a nasty surprise waiting for him.

Dakota Manhunt

Alan T. Leacroft

A Black Horse Western

ROBERT HALE · LONDON

© 1965, 2002 John Glasby
First hardcover edition 2002
Originally published in paperback as
Dakota Manhunt by Chuck Adams

ISBN 0 7090 7213 9

Robert Hale Limited
Clerkenwell House
Clerkenwell Green
London EC1R 0HT

Typeset by
Derek Doyle & Associates, Liverpool.
Printed and bound in Great Britain by
Antony Rowe Limited, Wiltshire

ONE
The Wild Ones

The group of men rode south-west out of Tucson just as dawn was greying the eastern horizon, the Matagorda Kid showing the way, his saddle tightened on a fresh mount, the Kid in it after less than three hours' sleep and a rest that had lasted only long enough for him to gulp down a plate of beans and meat at one of the eating houses in Tucson where no questions were asked and if eyebrows were raised at the sight of some of the men who slept and ate there, no mouths were ever opened. He was bone tired as he stared off into the grey half-light, but he rode without thinking about the weariness, because this was not something new for the lean-jawed man.

The previous evening, they had watched the train from the north steam into the railhead. It would wait there all night, leaving an hour after sunup for Vendado, some thirty miles along the single track line, and apart from the passengers, there were two sealed sacks containing more than fifty thousand dollars, cash for the miners and ranchers around Vendado.

At their first rest, beside a stream that ran swiftly in a splashing of white foam down from the summits of the tall hills, the Matagorda Kid related to the others his plans for holding up the train, how they would drop a couple of the tall pines across the track at the sharp curve some ten miles out of Vendado where the train was forced to slow for both curve and gradient and then take it from both sides.

They started bearing west in a wide circle. West was more open country, with scattered brush which would give them cover if necessary, but open enough for them to make good progress. Behind the Matagorda Kid, Haig Calton rode in silence. He had made no comment when the Kid had outlined his plans for taking the train, nor about the fact that there was likely to be a guard travelling with all of that money. He kept his innermost thoughts to himself, knowing that any argument would do no good and might even provoke the Kid. The other was shorttempered enough and although he considered himself to be fast with a gun, with at least fifteen dead men to prove it, he knew that the Kid was a shade swifter and at the moment had no desire to tangle with him.

Calton sat slouched a little in the saddle, a slightly-built, lean-hipped man, pale blue eyes never still, his wide-brimmed hat pulled low to keep the glaring sunlight out of his eyes. Everything about Calton seemed vaguely out of place, except for the expression on his face. Strictly, it was an absence of expression, a cold, strange emptiness which was almost frightening. The Kid had noticed it on several occasions, and it had come to him then that someday, somewhere, there might have to be a showdown between Calton and himself, unless one of them got it first.

Long before noon, they had reached a narrow strip of ground which overlooked the railroad track, the gleaming metal rails winding in a sharp curve almost directly below them, with the timber at this point reaching almost right down to the line. This was the spot which the Matagorda Kid had chosen. Now, sitting on his mount with a deceptive ease, he let his gaze roam over the scene spread out beneath him.

'We'll be able to get real close to 'em,' said the Kid thoughtfully. He squinted up at the sun to get an idea of the time. 'Better get that tree down across the tracks.' He pointed to one of the tall, slender pines that grew close to the rails.

Levin and Fleck stepped down from their horses, pulled the axes from their saddle thongs and climbed down the steep slope. The Kid watched them from beneath lidded eyes, then dismounted and walked across the small clearing to the tall outcrop of rock from where he was able to see all the way along the railroad, as far as the eye could see. At the moment, there was nothing to indicate that the train was on its way. The first sign they would have, would be the plume of black smoke close to the horizon where the gleaming rails vanished in the hazy distance. He rolled a cigarette from his tobacco pouch, lit it absently, drew the smoke deep into his lungs. From below him, there came the sharp sound of axes biting deep into wood. He turned his head then, watched the chips fly as the two men attacked the base of the tall tree, swinging the glittering axes in a smooth rhythm.

He felt oddly tensed and this was unusual for him, even before pulling something as big as this. Calton came over, stood behind him, staring out into the sunlit range. 'This is goin' to be big,' he observed, 'bigger than most of the other jobs we've done.'

The Kid glanced up, nodded. 'You checked back in Tucson that they were loadin' the money on board for this run?'

'Sure, sure, it's there all right.' Calton fell silent for a moment, his eyes speculative. 'I've been thinkin', Kid. About the guards. You got an idea for takin' care of them?'

'You've been thinkin'?' The Kid lifted his brows a little as he stared up at the other. His voice was soft, deadly quiet. 'I thought I did all the thinkin' around here.'

'I'll try to remember,' said Calton thinly. His voice was low, kept in control by an effort.

The Kid shrugged. He shifted himself into a more comfortable position on the rock. 'Forget the guards. We can take care of 'em. There will be two ridin' the locomotive and two more in the van carryin' the money. We take care of 'em first. Then go through the train, takin' all we can.'

'And then?'

The Kid grinned viciously. 'Then we pull out – fast. Back to the hide-out. We'll split the money and then lie low for a while.' His grin widened. 'I figure we can expect most of the lawmen in the State to be out huntin' us once they get word of this.'

There was a rending crash as the tree fell across the tracks, branches snapping under the impact. The kid nodded to himself in satisfaction. The driver of the locomotive would just see the obstruction as he was approaching the sharp bend in the tracks and would be forced to slow. Levin and Fleck began climbing the slope again, moving among the trees. The Kid dropped the butt of his cigarette on to the rock and ground it out with the heel of his boot.

'We should sight the train any minute now if it's on time,' Levin said.

'This is a good place,' muttered Bulmer tautly. He shaded his eyes against the sunglare, looked off to the east. The sun was reaching up to its zenith and the heat head was almost at the limit of its piled up intensity. Even in the green, aromatic shade of the pines, the Kid could feel it gathering about him, all of the moisture in his body rushing to the surface. He rubbed irritably at the sweat that formed on his forehead and began to trickle down his cheeks, mingling with the dust in the folds of his skin, itching intolerably.

The minutes dragged themselves by on leaden feet. Sitting a little apart from the others, Calton felt the sense of impatience growing in him with every second. Once he had his share of the money, he would leave this band of outlaws, ride south, far to the south, over the border and well into Mexico, where a man could be free, without the shadow of a bullet or the noose lying across his trail at every turn. He had been lucky in the past; fantastically so on several occasions, but already, somewhere at the back of his mind, was the realization that his luck was fast running out. If he did not die at the hands of the law, then it would be facing up to the Kid. He stole a sideways glance at the other, crouched against the flat rock that overlooked the wide, stretching valley down below them. A bad man to cross for all that he was so young. There had been times during the past few months when he had begun to wonder about the Matagorda Kid, where he came from, where he was going, and why he always seemed to be in so much of a hurry to get there, wherever it was. There were times when he wondered what it was that the other really wanted; for deep down inside, he had the conviction that the Kid was not in this for the money, but for something else. Excitement? Perhaps. The feeling of power it gave him to know that he was fighting the law of the whole state, that there was a price on his head? It was one way of gaining notoriety, of a place in the turbulent history of this State, but whether that was uppermost in the Kid's thoughts whenever he planned and carried through a robbery such as this, it was impossible to tell. His face told nothing. He never spoke of his past, of his life before he had become an outlaw. Certainly he was deadly fast with a gun, perhaps the fastest man that Calton had ever known, and such speed did not come without a great deal of experience.

For a long while, the men in the clearing were silent, some smoking, others lying back with their hats pulled down over their faces, surrendering themselves to the weariness that was in all of them. He shifted his gaze from the men, looked through the fringe of trees to where the long pine lay athwart the railroad tracks. It came to him then that the cowcatcher on the front of the locomotive might just be sufficient to clear the track of this obstacle if the driver decided to go ahead under full steam. If he was a nervous man, but alert, he might figure out that the tree had been dropped there for a purpose and decide to make a break for it.

He turned his head sharply, to find the Kid staring straight at him, a faintly amused smile curling his lips back from his teeth.

The Matagorda Kid said softly: 'You look worried, Haig. Somethin' on your mind?'

Calton shrugged. 'Just got the feelin' that maybe we should've blocked the track with somethin' a little more substantial than that pine. If that locomotive has a good head of steam, they might be able to drive that tree off the line without slackening speed.'

'We will,' the Kid said enigmatically. 'I've got that all figured out too.' He was getting to his feet even as he was speaking, moving across the clearing to where his horse was tethered. He lifted something from his saddle-bags. Calton looked more closely at the two bags the other carried, not having noticed them before.

'What's that?' Calton asked.

'Gunpowder,' said the other simply. 'Keep a sharp look-out for smoke on the horizon. Yell out when you see it.'

Carrying the two bags and the length of fuse, he scrambled down the rocky slope towards the fallen tree. Shale crunched, slid treacherously under his feet as he went down and in among the trees which bordered the track, it was very quiet.

It was the work of a few moments for him to dig the hole between the tracks, bury the bag in the soft soil, then attach the length of fuse before covering over the ground with a selection of the largest boulders he could find. At last, he was satisfied. Going to the edge of the track, he glanced up, then moved a few yards further to reach a point from where he could see the men among the trees. Abruptly, Calton lifted his hand, pointed to the east. The Kid nodded, more to himself than the other, yelled: 'Let me know when it's about half a mile away.'

Taking the box of sulphur matches from his pocket, he waited. Down here next to the track, the rising wall of rock and timber trapped the direct light and heat of the high noon sun, reflecting it down on him. He mopped his face with his bandanna, cursed the heat, aware of the growing sense of impatience in him. For the first time, he began to wonder a little about the men who rode with him. Was there a question mark against anyone? He shrugged the thought away. There was no time to think of that now, not with the train thundering along the track a bare mile away. Already, he could hear the moan of its whistle drifting in on the faint breeze.

'Light the fuse, Kid,' called Calton from the top of the rise. He waved his arm wildly.

Bending swiftly, the other struck one of the sulphur matches, placed it against the end of the fuse. It caught at once, sparked briefly, then began to smoke slowly along its snaking length. The Matagorda Kid waited for only a brief second before scrambling up the slope, feet sliding in the loose soil around the roots of the trees. The engine whistle blasted twice as he was halfway up the steep bank. Savagely, he thrust his way up with tremendous heaves of his legs. Then he was at the top, running for his mount. Jerking the Winchester from its scabbard, he checked that it was loaded, then motioned the rest of the men to take up their positions. He could make out the train now, slackening speed as it approached the curve. This was it, he told himself fiercely.

Then, as he watched the driver apply the brakes, he knew that the other had just spotted the obstruction on the line. Sparks flew from the wheels as the train began to slow. It was still travelling too quickly to pull up before it reached the fallen tree.

'Lucky you had that gunpowder,' grunted Calton harshly. He lifted his head to peer down through the bushes. 'She's goin' to plough right through that tree.'

'Could be that's what the driver is tryin' to do,'

muttered the other. He grinned faintly. The locomotive had begun to move around the bend now and the driver was clearly suspicious. The brakes were released and with a hissing of steam, the engine began to gather speed once more.

Then, with a savage roar, the gunpowder went up. Twisted pieces of metal lashed through the air. Slowly the smoke cleared. When the Kid was able to see again, the track had been torn up for a length of several yards by the titanic force of the explosion and a deep crater gouged out of the earth. Seconds later, unable to stop, the locomotive careened off the track, spun crazily sideways and turned over on to its side, steam hissing from the boiler. The car immediately behind twisted off the track, but miraculously, the others remained upright, grinding to a halt.

The driver of the locomotive and one of the armed guards had been thrown clear when the engine had over-turned. Both lay sprawled face downwards with their heads and limbs twisted at crazy angles, beside the track. Pulling up their neckpieces to cover their faces, the men leapt from cover, raced down the slope. Levin and Fleck ran for the steam-wreathed wreck of the locomotive. The Kid and Calton for the rear of the train. The others moved forward to prevent any trouble along the length of the stationary cars.

Swinging up on to the observation rail at the back of the last car, the Kid kicked open the door and moved inside, closely followed by Calton. He swung the Winchester to cover the guard, who had got to his feet and was in the act of moving towards the door.

'Stand quite still,' he hissed thinly, 'and don't make any move towards that gun.'

Behind the guard the uniformed man blinked in aston-ishment. He lifted his hands high above his head without being told. For a moment, the thought of action lived in the guard's eyes, his right hand, fingers spread wide, hovered close above the butt of the gun at his waist. Then he forced himself to relax, lifted his hands.

'That's better,' said the Kid quietly, his tone almost amused. He kept the two men covered with the rifle while Calton moved forward and removed their guns, tossing them through the window of the car.

'You won't get much by holding up this train,' said the guard tightly. 'We ain't carryin' anythin' you'd have any interest in.'

'We know what's in the express car,' the Kid told him, noticing the sudden change of expression that flickered across the other's face. 'There was plenty of talk in Tucson about the money you're carryin'. Now I suggest that you get it out and we'll soon be on our way.'

'You won't get away with this,' muttered the other.

'I think we will.' He turned to the express messenger. 'I reckon that you'd better get your keys and open up the door, or we'll be forced to blow it open with dynamite. If you reckon we won't, better take a look outside and see what's happened to the locomotive, or maybe you heard the explosion when we blew up the track.' One glance at the messenger's scared features was enough to tell the Kid that the other had. He was not to know that they had no more explosives left, that this was just bluff on their part.

'All right, all right, mister,' quavered the other. 'I'll open up. Ain't no cause for any more killin'.'

He took out his bunch of keys, moved to the far side of the car and turned one of them in the lock. The Kid motioned him forward, then the guard.

'Now both of you lie face downward on the floor,' he ordered. For a moment, the two men hesitated, then obeyed. Calton moved to the far end of the car, began to check through the registered mail, then turned sharply as the Kid called to him.

'What we're lookin' for won't be there, they'll have it locked away in the safe.' He went back and stood over the trembling figure of the express messenger. 'That's right, ain't it?'

The other swallowed, did not look up, but nodded his head quickly.

'Then I figure you'd better open it up, unless you want us to blow it open.'

'I don't have the keys to the safe,' protested the other. 'They don' allow us to carry them. The safe is only opened when we get to Vendado. Those are the rules and—' He broke off sharply as the Kid lowered the rifle until the end of the barrel was pressing into the small of the other's back, then he deliberately leaned his weight on it, while the other squirmed in agony.

'I'll give you until I count five to change your mind about that,' he said thinly, his voice hard. 'You may be a good employee of the railroad, but that isn't worth losin' your life for. One, two, three, four . . .' He increased the pressure on the rifle as he counted and the other suddenly yelled loudly. 'All right, I'll open it for you.'

'Now you're been' sensible,' the Matagorda Kid grinned. 'Get on your feet but don't try any tricks.'

He stood behind the other while the man opened the large safe, swinging the heavy metal door back. Calton whistled at what he saw. Three large boxes which rested on the shelf inside the safe. He kept a wary eye on the guard while the Kid dragged one of them out and let it drop on to the floor of the car. The wooden lid split under the force of the impact, scattering gold coin at his feet. Swiftly, he wrenched the lids off the other two. These contained paper money.

'Watch these two in case they decide to be heroes,' he said. Going to the door of the car, he fired the rifle twice into the air, the signal for Bulmer and Weller to come with the bags.

'You get anythin'?' Weller asked as he ran along the line to the open door of the car.

'Plenty,' said the Kid softly. He motioned to the three

boxes. 'Get them outside and hurry.'

'Yow!' said Bulmer, as he saw what the boxes contained. 'There must be over a hundred thousand dollars here.'

Ten minutes later the gold and paper currency had been taken from the train, the guard and messenger securely gagged and tied in the express car and the Kid and Calton went through the other cars taking everything they could find from the passengers. There were, unfortunately, few of these. Most of the west-bound passengers alighted at Tucson, very few continuing on the last lap of the journey to Vendado.

In the last car, there were only two passengers. One, a tall, beefy man was standing close to the window, trying to look out. He whirled as the two outlaws entered. The other passengers, a slightly-built man, with greying hair and a pair of rimless pince-nez balanced precariously on the end of his nose, seemed almost beside himself with fear.

'What is the meaning of this outrage,' roared the big man loudly.

The Kid walked forward slowly, not once removing his eyes from the other's face. He had left his rifle with Bulmer and now held a Colt balanced in his right hand. 'I'm sorry, gentlemen,' he said quietly, 'but this is a hold-up. If you'll hand over your valuables, nobody is goin' to be hurt.'

The big man stared at him with bulging eyes, the veins of his neck standing out under the tanned skin. 'I'll be damned if I will,' he said harshly.

The Kid bowed his head in mocking acknowledgment. 'You'll be dead if you don't,' he replied. There was the ominous click of the hammer being thumbed back as he spoke, the sound unnaturally loud in the stillness.

'You'll regret this, whoever you are.' The other's words fell into the silence like flakes of metal dropping into a deep, echo-ringing well.

The Kid prodded him with the barrel of the Colt,

thrusting him back against the side of the car. Reaching forward, he ran his hand over the other's black frock coat, felt the tell-tale bulge under the other's arm, and fished out the tiny, but deadly, derringer the other carried in the shoulder holster. Pulling the gold watch and chain out of the man's waistcoat, he thrust it into the bag which Calton carried, then proceeded to go through the prosperous looking man's pockets.

A few moments later, the other door to the car opened and Fleck came in, herding a tall, thin-faced man in front of him. 'This fella thought he'd try to be funny,' he said shortly. 'He was sittin' by himself in the other car.'

'You get anythin' from him'?' asked the Kid.

'A couple of hundred dollars. That's all. And this ring.' Fleck held out the ring which he had taken from the other's pocket. 'Looks like gold.'

'That ring belonged to my wife,' said the other harshly. 'It isn't worth much but it's all I have left of hers.'

'Sure,' sneered Fleck. 'You're breakin' my heart. They all say that.' He dropped the ring into the sack.

'Why you goddamned thief.' The other lunged forward, arms outstretched, caught at the neckpiece over Fleck's face and pulled it down, revealing the outlaw's features. Even as he stared at the other, Fleck reversed his revolver, clubbed the man savagely on the side of the head, at the same time, pulling up the neckpiece again, over the lower half of his face.

He swung sharply, the gun in his hand covering the other two men in the car menacingly. 'They all saw me,' he said tautly, speaking to the Kid. 'If they talk, they could—'

'Get out of here and back to the others,' ordered the Kid thinly.

'But if we let them live, they could put the finger on me,' protested the other.

'I said get out and join Bulmer with the horses.' There was steel beginning to show beneath the quietness of the other's tone.

For a moment, Fleck remained there, hesitant, his finger tight on the trigger. He paused to throw a quick glance at the unconscious man lying at his feet, then drew back one foot and kicked the other viciously in the small of the back before moving to the door of the car.

'Listen, Mister,' quavered the little man. 'We won't talk. Honestly we won't. I'm just here on business and I ain't seen that man before in my life.'

The Kid debated the position for a moment, inwardly cursing Fleck for his carelessness. Maybe this was what had been worrying him at the back of his mind ever since that moment when he had waited by the side of the track for the signal to light the end of the fuse. But it was done now. Fleck had been seen and that meant the end of him as a member of the band and—

There was the sharp bark of a rifle outside, a sound that cracked the stillness and echoed thinly along the walls of the canyon. Then another and a third; the signal for danger.

'Let's get out of here,' he said sharply to Calton. Addressing the two men, he added warningly: 'Stay inside and don't try to leave here for ten minutes. You understand?'

They nodded mutely, watched as the two men ran for the door of the car, out through into the next one, then down on to the track. As he ran, the Kid's eyes darted to the locomotive. Levin was running into the trees, one of the gunny sacks slung over his shoulder. Out of the corner of his eye, the Kid saw a hand thrust from the door of the splintered first coach, a hand that clutched a revolver, aiming it at the running man's back. Without pausing to think, he fired, saw the hand jerk back, the gun falling from bloodied fingers that suddenly dripped a red stain down the side of the splintered car.

At the top of the slope, Bulmer stood ready with the horses. He pointed through the trees as the Kid ran up to him. 'Riders headin' from the west,' he said harshly.

'About five miles away. They could've heard the explosion when you blew the tracks and decided to ride out for a look-see.'

The Kid nodded. His eyes moved across the wide stretch of ground to the west, almost immediately picking out the dust cloud which marked the position of the bunch of riders. They were forcing their mounts at a punishing pace, were evidently aware that there was something wrong.

'Let's go,' he said sharply. 'We'll be miles away from here by the time they reach the train and pick up our trail and we'll lose 'em in the brush.'

Swinging up into the saddle, he waited impatiently for the others to mount, then rode out through the trees, taking the narrow, twisting trail that led over the top of the ridge and down into the rough country on the northern side.

Half an hour later, in spite of the weight of gold and currency they carried, they were over the spine-crested ridge and riding swiftly through the mesquite-studded terrain that stretched clear to the range of low hills further to the north. A malignant branch of mesquite struck the Kid against his shoulder, twisting him sharply in the saddle, almost knocking him to the ground. The raking thorns tore along the horse's flanks, sending the animal bounding forward, smashing into chaparral, fighting, snorting madly, jerking its head high in an effort to avoid the thorny mass of vegetation. Several of the snaking branches tore across the Kid's shirt, but he ignored them. He could hear nothing from behind him, except the movement of the rest of the men and he guessed that the oncoming riders from the west had not yet arrived at the wrecked train. When they did, it would take them a little time before they located their trail and this chaparral and mesquite would undoubtedly force them to skirt the thorny growths.

They were deep in the mesquite now and he saw that it

was denser and thicker than he had anticipated, but there was no way of turning back now. They had to force their way through somehow. He straightened abruptly in the saddle, clamped a tight hold on the reins as the horse tried to swerve violently away from the torture of Spanish bayonet grass, the hard, spear points ripping and tearing at its flesh. Reeling in the saddle, he hung on with his knees, knowing that it would mean a serious injury if he was thrown into that mass of knife-edged points.

'Hell, we'll never get out of this,' growled Fleck hoarsely. He raked spurs along his mount's flank to urge it on at a greater speed.

'We'll make it.' The Kid turned slightly in the saddle, lips drawn hack over his teeth. He forced himself higher in the saddle, to obtain a better grip on the reins, sucking great gulps of air down into his lungs, aware of the red streaks of pain across his chest and neck where the barbs had torn the flesh.

The sun was beginning to lower down the arch of the heavens, throwing longer and darker shadows across the terrain by the time they rode into the low foothills of the range, plunging into the thickets which fringed the timber. A creek ran down the steep slope and it had gouged out a channel for itself in the soft earth, the vegetation rising high on both sides and curving over to form a complete arch above the stream, allowing only enough headroom there for a man on horseback to ride with his head lowered over the neck of his mount.

They splashed through the green tunnel, into a canyon, out at the far end, with the smooth rocky walls lowering on either side of them, coming into more open ground. Presently, there was a slow rise, broad and smooth and they slowed their pace as they began to climb.

A mile into the hills, with the crests pressing down on them from all sides and the slope steepened so that at last they were forced to dismount and lead the horses up, over short, sharp, razor-backed ridges and switchback courses, moving out of one rocky-bottomed canyon into another until finally they reached the narrow valley which nestled beneath the overhanging ridge almost at the top of the hills.

The old building of small logs stuck vertically in the ground had scarcely altered since the day it had been built, some time in the past, long before the war, when there had been prospectors ranging these hills in search of silver and gold. But the veins had been quickly worked out, the prospectors had left, leaving these tiny settlements scattered throughout the entire length and breadth of the range. There were a few sticks of rickety, homemade furniture in the shack, along with four iron beds ranged around the rear wall. Buck Standish already had a fire going and a thin curl of grey smoke issued from the metal chimney which was canted at a crazy angle from the sloping roof.

Tethering their mounts, the men went inside, dropping the gunny sacks near the door. The Matagorda Kid sank wearily on to a creaking stool, thrusting his legs out straight in front of him.

Buck filled a coffee pot and set it over the flames in a rock hollow. He threw a quick, questioning glance in the direction of the sacks. 'That information all right, Kid?' he asked meaningly.

The other nodded tersely. 'We must've got well over a hundred thousand dollars. There was a third box there with paper currency in it. We figured on only fifty thousand.'

'This is somethin' real big,' observed the other. He watched the coffee begin to boil. 'There'll be a big hunt after this.'

'We'll be safe enough here. We'll split the money and then lie low like we planned. Ain't no sense in' runnin' our luck too far.'

'How long you figurin' we gotta lie low?' asked Fleck. There was an odd edge to his tone.

'Depends. We can ride down into Vendado and snoop around in a few days.'

'Ain't you forgettin' that one of those *hombres* on the train recognized me, if not all three. Why didn't you let me shoot 'em down while there was still time? They can put the finger on me any time now.' His eyes narrowed a little. 'Or maybe you're goin' soft.'

The Kid tightened his lips. His gaze washed over the other's face like a wave of flame. 'That was your fault,' he grated thinly. 'You're too much of a liability for us now. Reckon that you'd better take your share of the money and ride, get as far away from here as you can, maybe across the border. That's where you've always had a hankerin' to go, ain't it?'

'Could be,' said the other slowly. 'But I mean to do that in my own good time. I don't intend bein' run out of the territory by three men like those. Besides, they're the only ones who can identify me. They'll still be in Vendado for a while, there won't be any trains runnin' back until they've got that track repaired. We could ride into town, pick 'em up and make sure they don't have a chance to pick me out.'

'Don't be a fool. Vendado is goin' to be swarmin' with law officers in the next few hours and any strangers ridin' into town will be closely watched.' Levin spoke up from the other side of the room, his tone caustic.

'Maybe so,' broke in the Kid, 'but there could be somethin' in what Fleck says. Our big advantage in the past has always been that we can ride openly into any town and pick up the information we need without any risk of bein' recognized. Thinkin' it over, I like the idea. There's only the one hotel in Vendado and they'll be sure to have put up there. We ride in, take them at gunpoint to someplace outside of town and silence them all – permanently.' His lips thinned in a grin as he nodded. 'Sure, I like that, Fleck. We'll pay those three *hombres* a visit tomorrow they won't be expectin'.'

Buck filled one of the rusted mugs with the hot coffee and handed it to the Kid. The other drank it down, felt it bring the warmth back to his weary body. When it was finished, he rolled himself a smoke, sat with his back to the wall, utterly relaxed. The rest of the men ate in silence, occasionally casting almost furtive glances towards the sacks near the door.

The Kid thought about the three men in the car of the train. There was no feeling in his mind at the knowledge that he had just pronounced a death sentence on all three. A man's life meant little to him. He weighed it against what it could do to him and if a man represented any danger at all, then he simply did not hesitate. The past years had made him both hard and vicious and yet there had been a time, long ago, when there had been nothing like this, when he had been able to ride any trail he chose with his head held high and with no fear of the law at his back. Each day had meant something new and good to him, but that was all lost now. No man could ever ride the same stretch of trail twice. There were some who claimed that he could always work his way back to it, but he doubted that. Certainly a man as deep in this business as he was had only one of two ways out – a bullet or a rope. At the moment, he fancied neither, yet there was, curiously, no thought in his mind that anything might go wrong when they rode into Vendado the next day; no sense that it might be the beginning of a fresh trail which could end in his death, in a way he could not possibly foresee.

TWO
The Matagorda Kid

Clint McCorg rode back into Vendado a little before sundown, tied his mount to the post in front of the sheriff's office and walked inside. He walked with the stiffness of a long day in the saddle, rubbed his shoulders as he tossed his wide-brimmed hat on to the desk and lowered himself into the high-backed chair behind it, stretching out his legs. Building himself a smoke, he lit the cigarette, and blew a cloud of smoke towards the ceiling, staring for a long moment at the glowing tip of his cigarette as if hypnotised. It felt good to be able to sit and not to have to think for a while, but to allow his taut limbs to relax.

Outside, in the street, he heard the rest of the boys ride in, rein up in front of the saloon and go inside with a lot of shouting. Well, they had deserved their drink, he reflected idly. It had been a long and dusty ride out there and back, and they had found mighty little to help them track down that outlaw band which had derailed the train and robbed it of close on a hundred thousand dollars. It was undoubtedly the biggest haul that anybody had got away with in this territory and he could visualise the pressure that would be brought to bear on him to round up this gang which had been operating in the territory for some time now, mainly holding up the stage which ran between Vendado and Tucson. Now, they had switched

23

their activities to the railroad. But how had they managed to discover that all that money would be on that particular train?

He thought about the descriptions which had been given him of the individual members of the band. Most of them would have fitted half the men in Vendado, himself included, he thought wryly. There had been only that positive identification from those three men in the front car, one of whom had stripped the neckpiece off one outlaw's face, getting a knock on the head for his pains. He rubbed his chin thoughtfully, the two-day growth of beard scratching under his fingers. Those men had been fortunate that they had not been killed. Since they could identify one of these men, it was surprising that the outlaws had not killed them there and then to prevent them from talking.

He felt hungry, but after he had finished his smoke, he went into the small room that opened off from the office and washed up, the mask of white alkali dust cracking on his face, coming away from his sun-scorched skin painfully. He had not realized that it had been so hot a day. In the excitement, the burning heat of the sun had passed unnoticed.

Walking over the street, he went into Chinese Charley's place, taking his usual seat near the single window, so that he could watch the door and the street at the same time.

'You look tired, Sheriff,' said Charley, as he came forward. 'You want the usual? Take five minutes.'

'That'll be fine, Charley.' He sat back, glancing through the window, thumbs thrust into his gunbelt, the jacket pushed back a little so that the last of the daylight glinted off the star pinned to his shirt. There was no one else in the eating house and with the emptiness, there was silence. The meal came and he ate slowly, Charley hovering in the background, his hands clasped in front of him.

'Is good?' he asked finally.

McCorg nodded. 'Just what I needed, Charley,' he acknowledged. 'It's been a long day and a longer afternoon.'

'There is some talk of the train being held up and robbed, Sheriff,' said the other hopefully, head cocked a little on one side. 'Is that true?'

'Afraid so. They got clean away with a hundred thousand dollars in gold and paper, as well as what they took from the passengers.'

'You find trail then, Sheriff.'

McCorg sighed. 'We found the trail, Charley, leadin' up towards that jungle behind the ridge. They must've ridden clean through it without stoppin'. Maybe had a look-out posted who spotted us ridin' up and gave the warnin'. Some of the passengers reckon they took off mighty sudden, so I guess that could have been it. But they had too much of a start on us. Maybe if we'd pushed our mounts through that chapparal and Spanish bayonet grass we might have had half a chance. But once they hit the hills, we'd never have been able to trail 'em there. It's been tried before whenever they held up the stage. There are a hundred different trails through those hills and a thousand different hidin' places where they could be shacked up right now.'

The other shrugged, but said nothing more, going back to the counter. He rested his elbows on it and stared inscrutably in front of him, thinking his own private thoughts.

McCorg ate the stew, dipping his bread into the gravy and wiping the plate clean that way. The coffee was hot, strong and black, and he drank two cups before pushing back his chair and getting to his feet. Tossing a couple of coins on to the bar, he went out, flicked the butt of his cigarette away into the middle of the street and moved away from the small restaurant. It was almost dark now, with long black shadows stretching across the street. The sun had long since dipped below the western horizon and the land was blue and cool all around the town, filled with the night smells of the distant hills in the breeze that blew along the main street. He crossed to the office, then paused in the middle of the street, still feeling the taste of the bitter alkali in his mouth and throat. He felt the need for the taste of whiskey to remove it and went instead to the saloon. The sound of raucous singing and laughter met him as he stepped inside. The men of the posse were at the card tables or ranged along the bar, hats tilted on the backs of their heads. No doubt they were boasting of what they would have done had things gone their way and they had caught up with the outlaw band. Things might have been different, he reflected idly, if that had really happened. From the scattered bits of information he had, they were a hard bunch of gunfighters and although they did not seem to kill for the sheer sadistic joy of killing as some of the outlaw gangs did, nevertheless if they were cornered they would undoubtedly give a good account of themselves.

He walked over to the bar, rested his weight on his elbows and lifted one finger, to the barkeep. Beside him, Menderer, the deputy gave him a sidelong glance. 'Figured you'd have been in here earlier, Clint,' he observed. 'The boys seem to be celebratin' some. Don't know what it is they're celebratin' though.'

'Probably the fact that we didn't run into that outlaw gang,' muttered the other dryly. He placed his fingers around the whiskey bottle as the barkeep made to take it away. 'Leave it there,' he said quietly.

'Sure, Sheriff.' The other nodded, pulled a wet cloth from under the counter and began methodically wiping away the round wet rings from the glasses on top of the bar.

'You got any idea who led this gang today?' asked Menderer, speaking out of the corner of his mouth.

'Your guess is as good as mine, but whoever it was, they sure knew what that express car was carryin'. First time the train's been stopped since the line was brought out here from Tucson six years ago, and the first time they was carryin' more than a few hundred dollars in gold or paper.'

'Some of the boys reckon it was the Matagorda kid pulled the job.'

McCorg shrugged. 'Could've been, I guess. But they usually work the stages. This doesn't quite fit in with their hold-ups of the past. Could be a different bunch altogether, but everybody will be ready to pin the blame on the Matagorda Kid.'

Menderer nodded. He drank his beer slowly, then set down the empty glass. McCorg nodded towards the whisky bottle. The other poured some of the amber liquid into his glass. 'What are you goin' to do about those three witnesses, Clint? You reckon they might know more than they told?'

'It's possible. That little fellow, Meekin, seemed scared enough to be keepin' somethin' back, but I doubt if either Finney or Stratford are the type to hold anythin' from us. They lost their valuables and now they're shoutin' for them back.'

'Not only them,' commented the deputy drily. 'Before we know it, the Governor will be down on our necks askin' for results. Things have been pretty lively around these parts for the past year or more. Even before you was elected sheriff, the Matagorda Kid had been holdin' up the stages, generally makin' a nuisance of himself. But this is the biggest haul yet and if he did it, and I for one reckon he did, then the sooner we lay him by the heels, the better.'

'Seems I've been hearin' nothing but the Matagorda Kid ever since I've been here,' McCorg mused. 'Could be that we've been tryin' to do things the easy way. If we was to take a posse up into the hills we might be able to smoke him out. If not, we could make things so hot for him he'd take it as time to move on.'

'Evidently you don't know those hills,' commented the

other, sipping the whiskey slowly. 'They're the best part of fifty miles long and thirty miles deep. How'd you expect a posse to cover all that territory? Besides, ain't it likely they got men keepin' watch on all the trails in and out of the hills. From up there on those ridges, they could spot anything bigger'n a coyote ten miles off. Even if they didn't set up an ambush for us, they could pull out long before we reached their hiding place. I tell you, Clint, it just ain't feasible.'

'I'm not so sure.' McCorg drained his glass, set it down on the bar and wiped his lips with the back of his hand. 'I've been thinkin' about those hills and their hide-out. They've shacked up in one of the old mining places.'

'And do you know how many of them there are likely to be in the hills?' inquired the other, lifting his brows a little.

'Quite a few, I guess.'

'You'd guess right, Sheriff. More'n fifty, all scattered among those rocks. It'd take you a lifetime to find 'em all, and what do you reckon that the Kid would be doin' while you were searchin' for him?' He shook his head. 'You don't stand a chance in hell.'

McCorg searched the other's face with a gaze that believed nothing. 'I think 1 know what I'm doin'. I want a posse to ride out with me at first light in the morning. Better warn the rest of the boys. I don't want to spoil their night, especially after the long ride this afternoon, but I reckon the sooner they get some sleep, the better.'

'They're not goin' to like it,' shrugged the deputy.

'Mebbe not. But they're still deputized until we catch up with these outlaws. I'll meet them outside the sheriff's office at dawn.'

Turning, not looking back to see whether his order had been carried out, he pushed open the saloon doors, stepped into the street. The first of the sky soldiers were beginning to show in the east where the sky had turned a deep purple with the oncoming night. Stepping along the boardwalk, he reached the main store just as Mary Kenner was locking the door. She turned quickly, gave him a warm smile as she recognized him in the darkness.

'Clint! I heard that you'd ridden out of town after that band of outlaws who robbed the train. What happened? Did you manage to catch up with them?'

He shook his head, took her arm. 'Afraid not, Mary. They must've seen us ridin' up and lit out for the hills. I'm takin' a posse out tomorrow morning to try to track them down.'

'Be careful. Dad was saying that they're the same band that held up the stages nearly a year ago. There's talk in town.' She brushed a stray curl back from her forehead.

'You going home, Mary?'

The girl nodded, turning her head to took up at him in the gloom. 'When did you get back into town?'

'About an hour ago. Just before sundown.'

They started walking along the hollow-echoing board-walk, steps in unison. The buildings on that side of the street were soon left behind and the night closed in about them, a night filled with the chirping of crickets and the faint, far-off wail of a prairie dog out in the desert to the north-west.

'It's a beautiful night,' Mary said softly. 'The stars seem so close I could almost reach up and touch them with my fingers.'

'There'll be a moon soon,' he said, looking off to the east where a faint, pale-white glow lay close to the horizon, picking out the undulating silhouette of the hills.

Turning off the end of the boardwalk, they stepped down on to the grassy earth, walking slowly towards the thin fringe of trees, beyond which the yellow lights of several houses flickered through the branches.

Beneath the trees, Mary stopped, laid her hand on his arm. 'One of the men from the train came into the store just before we closed and he was saying that somebody got a good look at one of those outlaws.'

'That's true.'

'Then don't you think it possible that they might try to keep those men quiet?'

McCorg pondered that for a moment, then shook his head slowly. 'I doubt it. If they had intended to kill them because they might recognize one of their number, they had their best opportunity back there on the train. Yet they rode off without harming any of them. I reckon those three men are quite safe here in Vendado.'

She looked up at him suddenly. 'How can you possibly be so sure of that?' Her face was flushed a little now, glancing at McCorg who had been smiling faintly at her seriousness, but whose face now bore a frown, lips drawn tightly together.

'I can't be absolutely certain,' he said defensively. 'But—'

'But you're willing to risk their lives because you think you may be right.'

She sounded angry and he hesitated for a moment, a little unsure of himself. For a moment, he remained silent, then said slowly and deliberately. 'Those outlaws have run for cover to their hide-out in the hills. I aim to smoke them out as soon as it's light tomorrow. That's the best defence these three witnesses have got, I reckon. If we just sit around here in town twiddlin' our thumbs, they'll strike again and we'll still be no closer catchin' them and bringin' them to justice.'

'Clint, those three men can be in terrible danger,' she went on pleadingly. 'You know as well as anybody that this band somehow got the information about that gold shipment and the only place they could have got it would have been in Tucson.'

Clint smiled now. 'You figure this all out by yourself, Mary?' he asked.

'Of course not. I'm not the law around here. Father reckons that since nobody has ever seen the faces of this band, until today, they could ride into any town without being recognized, pick up the local gossip and then make their plans for robbing the stage line or the railroad.'

'Your father explained this to you?'

'Most of it. I suppose it's only common sense.'

McCorg said quietly: 'What he says is true. But it's all the more reason why we should track them down as soon as possible.' He glanced thoughtfully through the trees to where the moon, round and full and yellow, was just lifting clear of the black peaks standing out on the eastern horizon. 'But I think I've kept you out talkin' too long, Mary. Try not to worry about those men. Leave all of the worryin' to me, that's what I'm bein' paid for.'

Mary did not answer, but moved slowly through the trees, up the porch steps and into the house. The door closed softly behind her and McCorg paused there for only a moment before turning and going back towards the quiet town. He noticed that there was very little sound issuing from the saloon now, that most of the horses which had been tethered outside were gone. He guessed that Menderer had passed on his message. Going into the office, he turned down the light and stretched himself out wearily on the bunk in the corner, lay with his hands clasped behind his neck as he stared up at the ceiling, listening to the faint night noises outside. This was a hell of a thing to have happened, he thought tiredly. Even Mary thought that he was doing the wrong thing and there was no mistaking how Menderer and the rest of the men he had deputised the previous day were feeling about the position.

They rode north-west out of Vendado, cutting through the rocky stretch of trail and then out into the mesa. The sun was just showing over the ragged peaks to the east and everything was still in virtual shadow with the air holding a little of the coolness of the night. A couple of black cypress trees, standing on the side of the trail, lifted like tall sentinels against the faint sunglow from the peaks. The day was becoming brighter as the sun rose.

Beside McCorg, Menderer rode in silence, sitting tall in the saddle, peering in every direction. He had made no comment since they had pulled out of town, but McCorg could see that there was still something troubling him.

They rode until by mid-morning, they came within sight of the railroad and followed it until it swung in a wide circle, heading back east to Tucson. At the point where the robbery had taken place, they found the locomotive and two cars still there. The others had been coupled to another locomotive from Tucson and hauled back there to clear the line as much as possible. Turning in the saddle, as they rode past, Menderer said sourly: 'It's goin' to take them some time to clear and repair that part of the track.'

'Maybe by that time we'll have caught the coyotes responsible,' muttered one of the men, laughing harshly.

McCorg nodded thoughtfully, not joining m the general laughter at the other's remark. 'They're up yonder someplace,' he said thinly. 'All we have to do is smoke them out.'

'I keep tellin' you that you don't have a chance,' Menderer said. 'Sheriff Clelland rode into those hills on their trail, not once, but a dozen times, after they'd held up the stages, but he never saw hair nor hide of 'em. We won't have any better luck, I'll wager.'

'Let's wait until we get there and see,' McCorg murmured. He felt a faint surging of anger against the other. More because of the fact that he was becoming unable to escape the truth of what the other said, than because of his continual harping on the point. But out here, at least, they were doing something constructive and when word did come down from Tucson, asking what was being done, there would be something to report. But he did not feel as sure of himself as he tried to appear to the others.

They breasted a low rise. In front of them stretched the jungle of Spanish bayonet grass and chapparal, with tall mesquite bushes interspersed at intervals through the spiking vegetation.

'You goin' to ride through that?' asked Menderer, pointing.

'No. We'll skirt around it. That way will add an hour or so to the ride, but it will be easier on the horses.'

Two hours on the trail across dusty alkali with the heat head lifting around them and the sunlight glaring in their eyes. White dust worked its way between their clothing and skin, harsh and abrasive on their flesh. It mingled with the sweat that dripped from their foreheads into their eyes, and trickled down the folds on their cheeks. Tenseness came to the men as they rode. They were now approaching the foothills that lifted from the flatness of the plain, rocky at their base, with the timber line beginning about three hundred feet up.

These were hard men now working at a hard trade; riding out on the trail of killers and robbers. Men who knew they had to be hard, fast on the draw, to keep alive if they should come up against the men they were hunting. They had ridden under a few sheriffs – had known some who were brutal slave-drivers, men in fact who were little different from the killers they sought. But this man was different.

Here was a man who had obviously lived with violence for a long time; a man who could build a situation to force a point. If he had to, McCorg would force these men to ride with him throughout the whole length and breadth of these wide hills to hunt down these killers. Yet even Menderer, who thought that he knew the other better than most, believed that he would not do so simply because they had robbed the train. The men who had been killed, had died because of the explosion which had thrown the engine and the next car off the track. Nobody had been shot during the hold-up, although several men had been wounded.

There was silence now except for the harsh breathing of men and horses. McCorg reined up his mount as he faced the rocks which lay in front of them. Lifting his head, he peered up into the tall trees that grew thickly along the lower slopes, pushing his sight as far as possible into the dense green undergrowth which grew around them, then staring even higher, as far as the towering razor-backed ridges immediately beneath the crests, seeking the flash of sunlight off the barrel of a rifle, any telltale sign that would indicate the presence there of a man watching them from a vantage point above them. Finally, he looked down, rubbed his eyes as they smarted from the harsh sunglare.

'See anything?' asked Menderer.

McCorg shook his head, lips pursed into a tight line. 'Nothin' there,' he murmured. He twisted in the saddle, looked back at the men who followed him. He said tautly: 'Keep your eyes open now and be ready for trouble. We'll ride in single file, with five yards between each man so that if trouble does start, we can deal with it. That understood?'

There was a low murmur of voices. The men nodded their heads. They touched the butts of their guns with absent movements, faces tight, strained. McCorg noticed the expressions, knew what they meant. But there was no turning back now. He threw a swift glance at Menderer. 'You ready?' he asked.

'If you mean to go through with this, then I'm ready.' The deputy's tone was low and steady.

Clint McCorg leading, they rode into the rocks, splashed over a wide stream that ran over a smooth-stoned bed. The stream, born high among the rocks, ran swiftly here and their horses breasted the current as they swung them a little upstream for better footing. McCorg felt his own mount stagger as the water began to push against its chest, come to a full pause for a moment to regain its balance, and move on again, stumbling as it clambered up the far bank. The trees shouldered their way right down to the narrow trail at this point and for the first time, he felt a faint sense of apprehension, knowing that if an ambush had been laid anywhere along the trail that wound its way up to the higher ridges and peaks, the bushwhackers would be able to bring a solid volley of fire to bear on them before they were even aware of their presence.

But there was no chance of turning back now. In places, the trail was so narrow that they were forced to ease their mounts through thick vegetation, with clawing branches snaking down at them from both sides, hemming them in, raking long, thorny fingers across their faces and arms, and along their horses' flanks. McCorg tried to crouch lower in the saddle to avoid most of the overhanging branches, ducking blindly when great creepers, as thick as a man's arm, appeared out of nowhere, swinging at him without warning.

Then, almost before he was aware of it, the trees thinned, fell behind them and in front of him, the long, bare rocks which jutted out from the slopes bordering the trail, were clean and clear in the morning sunlight and he could hear the faint, shrill cries of birds among the trees they had just left.

The empty rocks stretched for a long distance in front of them, picking up the heat and glare of the sun, throwing it back at them in dizzying waves. An occasional lizard streaked in a flash of purple from one rock to another and once, he saw one sunning itself on a flat rock, less than ten feet from a coiled rattler that stirred itself with a deceptive laziness as they rode by.

Keep your mind on the cries of the birds, he told himself tensely; if there is anybody around these rocks, or among the trees, they'll give you plenty of warning.

Half an hour later, they swung around a bend in the trail and came in sight of a couple of small wooden shacks built in against a sheer wall of rock that towered over them, threatening to crush them beneath its massive weight. With a sharp, sudden movement, McCorg reined up his mount, leaned forward and withdrew the Winchester from its scabbard, levered a shell into the breech, sat ready. There was no sign of movement, no sound and the scene held an air of desolation which could be easily felt as well as seen.

Menderer gigged his mount forward until he was beside McCorg. 'Ain't been anybody near this place for ten years or more,' he observed.

'You could be right,' nodded McCorg. He let his gaze wander over the rock which backed the two buildings. There had been rock slides here and he could see where one of them, probably the most recent, had crashed down and caved in the rear of the nearer building, the wood smashed and splintered under the onslaught. Kneeing his horse, he walked it forward, sitting balanced easily in the saddle, the rifle held in his right hand, his finger tight on the trigger, ready to loose off a shot at the first sign of danger.

Slipping from the saddle, he moved towards the half-open door of the nearer shack, paused for the barest fraction of a second and then kicked it open with the toe of his boot, sending it crashing inward. Inching forward, body pressed against the wall, he threw a quick glance inside. Dust lay white and undisturbed on the floor and a moment's examination was enough to show him that Menderer had been right. He stepped out into the bright sunlight again.

Thrusting the Winchester back into its scabbard, he nodded. 'This ain't the place, that's for sure,' he remarked. 'Let's move on.'

The sun passed its zenith as they made their way upgrade, moving along the narrow switchback courses that led them higher into the hills. Midway through the afternoon, they rode into a wide plateau, came within sight of another old mining site.

McCorg sat still eyeing it closely. It looked no different from the other one they had located, nothing there to tell them that it was being used as the hide-out of the outlaw gang, yet they could not afford to take any chances. He motioned the men from their saddles, slid to the ground.

'Well, what do you think?' asked Menderer.

The other shrugged. 'Hard to say. We're below the shack. If we could get above it, we might be able to see any tracks. Get the men to scout around and see if they can find anything, while you and me try to figure out a way of getting up there without bein' potted by anybody who might be hidin' inside that cabin.'

'Somethin' here, Sheriff,' called one of the men, pointing.

McCorg went over to the other. The tracks of horses were clearly visible in the dust among the rocks leading up to the shack.

'They look new,' he said, going down on one knee. 'Now where are they now? I'd say there were at least half a dozen men here, possibly more.'

'They're evidently not up at the shack right now.'

'No, but they could've left one man there on guard.' McCorg stood up, threw a swift glance in the direction of the shack. He made himself become calm and sucked a deep breath in through his teeth.

Waving the rest of the men forward, he stationed them in a line with their rifles to cover Menderer's and his advance. They kept their eyes fixed on the front of the shack as they toiled their way slowly up the slope, moving an inch at a time through the loose dust that shifted treacherously under their feet. The long board of the shack seemed bleached by long exposure to the hot sun, and at that distance it seemed deserted, no sign of life or movement in the doorway or the windows on either side.

They still had thirty yards to go and McCorg felt the sweat start out on his forehead and begin to trickle down into his eyes, half blinding him. He rubbed angrily at it with the back of his left hand, squinting into the flooding sunlight.

'There's someone there,' muttered Menderer from the side of his mouth. He did not once remove his gaze from the wooden cabin as he spoke. 'I'd swear I saw something move just inside the doorway.'

'You sure?' McCorg went down on one knee behind a rock. It seemed too quiet here. There was a different kind of feeling compared with that he had experienced when he had moved up to that other shack. He tested the shadows inside the building, searching closely for any movement there, no matter how slight. He could make out nothing. If there was anyone hiding there, watching their slow approach then he was staying low, out of sight.

'Damn it, Sheriff, I ain't sure of anythin' right now,' whispered the other.

'All right. I'm goin' to make a run for that horse trough. Stay here and keep me covered. Got that?'

'Be careful. If there is someone through that door, he could pot you easily before you make it to cover.'

'That's a chance I'll have to take. Just make sure you ain't slow with that rifle. That's all I ask.'

He drew up his legs under him, tensing the muscles of his thighs. Arching his back, he clutched the Colt tightly in his right hand, breathed deeply for half a dozen breaths, then kicked off and darted forward, head low to present a more difficult target, sprinting towards the long wooden horse trough as quickly as he could. Almost at once, a rifle shot from the shack blew the silence apart. There came a second lancing spurt of flame before he flung himself down behind the trough, rolling over on to his side, twisting to catch a brief glimpse of the position of the gunman. He was crouched down behind the window to the left of the door. Snapping off a couple of shots, he wriggled into a more comfortable position, drew in his partly exposed legs. Another shot blasted from the shack. A long splinter of wood was torn from the edge of the trough, sent slicing through the air close to his head. Menderer loosed off a couple of rapid shots which did no damage, then silence fell around the shack, thick and ominous.

Now, thought McCorg grimly, we'll see how good this hombre is. We can wait him out and if he hasn't got good nerves, or patience, he'll crack sooner or later, most likely before it gets darks because he knows we can then move in on him and take him from three sides. And if he's waiting for the rest of the gang to turn up, he's wasting his time. We can take them easily with our numbers. No doubt he's already figured that too, knowing that we'll be watching the trails now that we've tracked down their hide-out.

Out of the corner of his eye, he watched Menderer. The deputy was lying on his stomach behind the rock, the long barrelled Winchester thrust out in front of him, eyes fixed on the shack. There was no possible way by which the man in there could get away, except by the door or the windows. They had him pinned down completely.

He crawled along on his elbows until he reached the end of the trough, risked a quick glance around it. The movement brought no response from the shack. Either the other had not spotted him, or he was not intent on wasting his ammunition. Studying the ground thoughtfully, he settled down on his chest, eyes narrowed. The rest of the posse were still in position at the lower end of the slope.

Let the silence work on the other, he reflected. Unless he's very good, he'll soon betray himself, maybe begin firing recklessly, in the hope that if he loosed off sufficient shots, some were bound to hit their target, maybe he would try to make a run for it into the rocks that lay in tumbled heaps to one side of the shack. Maybe he would just squat there in the shack and try to outwait them. Time passed slowly and the silence began to drag. There was a soft, half-heard sound as Menderer, a few yards away, shifted his body into a more comfortable position. McCorg could feel the clutching fingers of cramp work their way through the muscles of his legs and body, lancing into him. He forced himself to ignore them. He was used to this. Patience made a rock out of him, forced him into immobility.

It was less than an hour later, although to McCorg it seemed longer, when a harsh voice from the shack yelled: 'Better ride on, Sheriff, and take those men with you. The rest of the boys will be back soon and then you'll never get out of these hills alive. Think it over, McCorg.'

Clint felt a faint shock at the use of his name, but it subsided rapidly. The other had possibly recognized him when he had made that run for the trough.

'You ain't scaring us,' McCorg called back. 'We know you're alone in there and with the men I've got at my back, that gang of yours won't dare to attack us. Now that we've found your hide-out, this is the end of the trail for all of you.'

'If you're such a goddamned good lawman, walk out of there and meet me man to man.'

McCorg grinned viciously to himself. He said nothing, easing himself forward to rest his shoulder against the warm wood of the trough.

'Damn you, lawman,' grated the other, after a long pause. 'I always did have you men reckoned as cowards. You're nothin' but a bunch of women, scared to come out and fight in the open.'

That's right, McCorg thought to himself. Get yourself really worked up and then maybe you'll do something rash and we'll really nail you.

There was a longer pause this time. Then, abruptly, he spotted the movement at the window, lifted the Colt as he saw the man's hat lift above the ledge. Almost, his finger tightened on the trigger, then he forced himself to relax. The hat had tilted at an angle and he knew it was balanced on the barrel of a rifle. The hat stayed there for a long moment and then, when it failed to draw a single shot, it vanished out of sight. Leaning back, McCorg threw a quick glance at the sky. The sun had passed its highest point, was sliding swiftly down the western arch of the heavens, the shadows were lengthening and the narrow valley in which they were, grew progressively darker as time went on and the sun began to slip away behind the towering peaks.

McCorg could feel the tension growing inside him, tightening the muscles of his arms and chest. He tried to relax, but it was impossible to do so. The sweat on his limbs caused his clothing to stick to his skin, irritating and chafing with every slight movement he made. His breath sighed in and out of his lungs and made small whistling sounds as it was expelled through his tightly clenched teeth. Cramped and waiting, he lifted the Colt, fired a couple of shots at the window where he had seen the flash of the rifle. Chips of wood, dagger-like, lifted into the air as the slugs tore into the ledge. The answering fire was almost immediate. Dust spurted up from the ground beside the trough as slugs ploughed into it. He withdrew his head sharply, then squirmed to one side, motioned the men at the bottom of the slope to move up.

A solitary rifle shot hammered from the shack, but it was the only one the hidden outlaw was able to fire before a volley from Menderer and McCorg forced him to keep his head down. From the edge of his vision, McCorg saw a small bunch of his men run forward along the face of the cliff beside the shack, approaching it from the side. They were now safe from any fire from the front of the shack.

'You're surrounded,' McCorg yelled harshly. 'Better come on out with your hands lifted. I don't intend to give you another warning. Ten seconds and we come in shooting.'

'*Come on in and try to take me, lawman!*'

Another shot fractured the wood near his head, forced him to push himself hard into the dirt. But now, McCorg was thinking ahead to eventualities. He accordingly aimed carefully, pumped three quick shots into the window behind which the outlaw crouched. There came a loud cry from the shadows inside the building, and no further shots.

Menderer came running forward, threw himself down on the ground beside McCorg. 'Think he's hit?' he asked harshly.

'Could be a trick. Wait for the rest of the boys to move up. Then we'll close in on him. He doesn't have a chance now and he knows it.' He smiled to himself in the growing dimness, but was still acutely aware of the tension inside him.

Within minutes, there was a ring of men around the shack. McCorg got his feet under him, knowing they were waiting just for his signal. Gritting his teeth, he fired off a single shot, then ran forward, legs slipping in the dust, the deputy close on his heels. As he ran, he brought up his Colt, saw the shape just inside the door, glimpsed the gun barrel being lined up on his chest. Then he squeezed off a single shot, the muzzle blast a blue-crimson in the gloom.

The man inside the doorway staggered as the slug hit him, half turning him under the bone-shattering impact. His gun blasted a split second later, the bullet striking ground more than three feet from McCorg. Already, the other was falling forward. Somehow, he found enough strength to squeeze the trigger once more, but the barrel was pointed downward and the slug hit the dirt just in front of his own feet as he fell.

McCorg went down on one knee beside the fallen man as the others rushed up, their guns drawn. 'He's dead,' he said a moment later, looking up. 'A pity. He might have been forced to tell us where the rest of the gang is.'

'He died poorly,' said Menderer. 'What do we do with him. Bury him?'

'Reckon that it's the only decent thing to do in the circumstances. A couple of you move back down the trail, keep a sharp look out for the rest of the gang in case they come ridin' up. Anybody recognize this *hombre*?'

The men shook their heads as they stared down at the dead man's face. The deputy said: 'Never set eyes on him in my life.'

'Probably he stays here to look after the loot.' McCorg

nodded as a fresh thought struck him. 'We'll look around for that once we've got him under the ground. Could be they brought it back here and hid it someplace.'

THREE
High Noon Murder

The small group of men rode into the northern end of Vendado a little after ten o'clock. Already, the sun was up in a cloudless sky and the dust devils eddied along the street. The men tied their horses to the hitching rail outside the saloon, went inside. At the same time, another group of them rode into town at the southern end of the main street, walked their mounts through the middle of Vendado, and put up at the Trail's End saloon, a short distance from that in which the others were, and almost directly across from the hotel, the only two-storied building at that end of town.

Leaning against the bar, the Matagorda Kid said quietly to Levin: 'The others are here. I saw their horses outside the far saloon. They'll make sure there's no trouble from anyone in the street while we go inside and find those three *hombres.*'

'You're almighty sure that they'll be in the hotel,' muttered the other.

'At this time of the mornin', it ain't likely they'll be anyplace else. I didn't see any sign of them on the street as we rode in and Calton and the others obviously didn't, otherwise they'd have given us a signal.'

'You just figurin' on strollin' across to the hotel and fetchin' them out at gunpoint?' The other gulped down

44

his whiskey, set the empty glass on the bar, made to pour himself another from the nearby bottle, then stopped as the Kid's fingers curled tightly about his wrist, squeezing hard.

'No more,' said the other harshly. 'We got work to do and I don't want any slip-ups.'

'Where'd you reckon the sheriff is right now?' asked the other, lips drawn into a tight line.

'Judgin' from the dust we spotted on the trail, I reckon he's out lookin' for us.' There was a beat of harsh amusement on the other's tone.

Levin nodded, giving him a narrow stare. He knew that the Kid was, in all probability, right in this assumption. They had caught sight of the dust cloud on the trail across the desert while they had been riding the timberline and although the bunch of riders had been too distant for them to identify any of them, there was little doubt as to who they were. In confirmation of this, there was the fact that very few horses were tethered to the trail posts along the street and the sheriff's office had appeared deserted when they had ridden slowly past. Still, there was one way of finding out.

He crooked his finger at the barkeep. The other came forward, eyed the bunch of men closely, but with no expression on his pudgy features. His gaze had dropped momentarily to the guns the men carried, slung low at the waist, the butts worn smooth from long use.

'Place seems pretty quiet today,' Levin said softly. 'Where is everybody?'

'You boys must've just ridden into town,' said the other after a brief pause, 'we got ourselves a little excitement yesterday. A bunch of outlaws held up the train not far from town, took nearly a hundred thousand dollars, they reckon.'

'That where the sheriff is?' queried the Kid, looking directly at the barkeep for the first time. 'We rode past the jailhouse, but there was no sign of life.'

'Rode out with a posse just before dawn this morning,' went on the other expansively. He rubbed at the top of the bar with the cloth tied to his waist. 'Don't figure he'll catch 'em now. They'll probably be clear across the border by now with all of that money. I figure it should keep 'em happy for life.'

The Kid lifted his brows a little, nodded, drawing his shoulder blades together. 'Guess we missed the excitement,' he affirmed.

'You fellows goin' to be in town long, or just ridin' through?'

'We figure on stayin' if we like the place,' said the Kid easily. He jerked a thumb towards the door. 'That the only hotel you got in town?'

'That's right. Plenty of room though. We ain't got many visitors here at the moment. Just one or two from the train, waiting to move on out of here. Some left by the stage half an hour ago. Guess the others will have to do that too, if they want to leave soon. It'll be a week or more before they fix that line out of town.'

The Kid pursed his lips. He had not figured on anybody leaving on the stage, and it might be that those three men they were seeking had already left Vendado. If that was the case, then the sooner they discovered it and took off after that stage, the better. He finished the whiskey, nodded almost imperceptibly to the men ranged along the bar, turned and walked towards the door.

They made their way slowly across the street. On the boardwalk immediately in front of the hotel, the Kid paused, turned his head casually and glanced along the dusty, sun-hazed street. There was a bunch of men lounging outside the other saloon and he noticed Calton standing there, a cigarette dangling from his lip, the smoke curling up around his face. The other inclined his head a little as he saw the Kid watching him. He thrust his thumbs into his gunbelt and leaned his shoulders against one of the wooden uprights.

'All right,' murmured the Kid softly. He went inside the hotel. In the lobby there was a welcome coolness, so different from the growing heat outside. Walking between a double row of potted ferns, he moved to the desk. The clerk glanced up from the paper he had been reading, eyed the men standing there with a renewed interest.

'What can I do for you, gentlemen?' he asked.

The Matagorda Kid took out the card which he had taken from one of the wallets he had removed from the men on the train. 'We're friends of Mr Finney,' he said. 'I understand he's staying here. Could you tell us whether he's in and the number of his room?'

The clerk raised his brows a little, but said nothing, bending his head over the book in front of him, studying it closely, with an almost exaggerated care.

'Finney,' he murmured, half to himself, running his finger down the list of names on the page. 'Ah yes, he booked in yesterday. I believe he was on that train which was held up outside of town.'

'His room number?'

'Number thirty-four. At the top of the stairs and along the corridor facing you.'

'Do you know if anyone else from the train is staying here?'

The clerk consulted the register once more, nodded: 'Two more. They're in the rooms on either side of Mr Finney's.'

'Thanks,' said the Kid. He started for the stairs. 'Don't bother to come up. We'll find them.'

Catfooted, they made it along the corridor. Fortunately, all of the doors were closed and the Kid paused outside number thirty-four, then motioned the others to the rooms on either side of it. 'No noise,' he said. 'Just get them out of there and into the corridor.'

He waited until the others were in position, then rapped loudly on the door. For a moment nothing happened, then he heard heavy footsteps approaching. A pause, and the door opened. The burly figure of Finney stood framed in the opening. Over the other's shoulder, he saw the two men seated at the table in the middle of the room. Meekin was there, staring straight ahead of him, cards held in his right hand. Facing him across the table was the third member of the trio, Stratford.

'No need to bother with those other rooms,' the Kid called quietly. 'They're all gathered together in here.'

'Now see here,' blustered Finney. 'Just what is the meaning of this. Can't a few men have a quiet hand of poker without—'

He broke off sharply as the Kid slid the Colt from its holster and jabbed him painfully in the ribs, forcing him back into the room. 'Just keep quiet,' he ordered and motioned the other towards the table, 'and warn those others to keep their hands flat on the table where I can see them. If either tries to go for a gun or makes a move I don't like, you'll be the first to die.'

The Kid saw the other swallow thickly, and little beads of sweat popped out on his forehead and upper lip. He ran a suddenly dry tongue around his mouth as he backed away.

'Just who are you?' he demanded hoarsely. 'And what do you want with us?'

'Let's say that we met before and it could be that you represent a menace to at least one of us. We decided therefore to ride into town and rectify matters.'

'This is that gang that held up the train yesterday,' said Meekin in a high, quavering voice. 'I'd recognize that tone anywhere.'

Stratford's eyes were on the Kid, but he said nothing. He let the cards he held fall one by one on to the table in front of him.

'What do you intend to do with us?' Finney asked finally.

'You're comin' for a little ride with us,' the other said softly, very soft. 'We figure it would be unwise to leave you here in town where you could go running to the sheriff as soon as he rides back. You see, we've always had the big advantage so far of bein' able to ride into any town and never be recognized, because nobody has seen our faces whenever we've held up a stage or train. But one of you acted very foolishly yesterday, gave away the identity of one of us and we have to make sure that it remains a secret.'

'They're goin' to kill us,' said Meekin in a shrill voice. He pushed back his chair, half rose to his feet, then collapsed in a shaking heap as Levin turned his gun on him. 'Better sit quite still,' Levin said warningly. 'I've got an itchy trigger finger here and although I don't want to have to kill you here, I will if I have to.'

'You'll never get away with this,' snarled Finney hoarsely. 'As soon as the sheriff gets back into town, he'll hunt you down. How far do you reckon you'll get, even if you do kill us in cold blood?'

'We'll get far enough,' the Kid said. 'Don't worry about that.' He glanced at Levin. 'Shuck them for guns,' he said quietly. When the other had searched the three men, tossing the Colt which Meekin carried and the two small Derringers the other two men carried in shoulder holsters on to the bed in the corner of the room, he said: 'That's all they're carryin' '

'Get movin' then.' The Kid's face resumed its tautness. He gestured with the Colt towards the door. 'You'd all better move easy and not make any funny move. I'll shoot the first man who does that in the back. And if you're expectin' any help from the townsfolk, there's somethin' you ought to know. The sheriff and a posse have ridden out lookin' for us and they won't be back in town much before nightfall. Another thing, too, I've got men stationed on the other side of the street, just itchin' to join in if anybody decides to be heroic.'

He noticed the fractional slump of Finney's shoulders at these words, knew that the big man had almost certainly been banking on trying to make a run for it once they were out in the street. A cold smile twisted the Kid's lips as he ushered the three men down the stairs and into the lobby of the hotel. He kept his hand close to the holstered gun at his side, moving close behind Finney and Meekin.

The clerk glanced up idly from behind the desk. 'Everythin' all right, Mr Finney?' he asked.

Finney cleared his throat, then nodded quickly as the Kid stepped closer to him. 'Sure, sure, everything's fine,' he said hoarsely. 'Fine.'

'You comin' back durin' the day?'

'Yes, I reckon so. Probably be back for supper.'

'I'll see somethin' is kept for you in case you're late,' nodded the other. He buried his head in the paper once more, took no further interest in the proceedings.

Meekin, moving through the doors of the hotel first was pale and sweating as he emerged into the sunlit street. The Kid noticed the other's lip was trembling as he hesitated on the edge of the boardwalk, teetering on one foot, staring up and down the street, evidently looking for the slightest chance to get help. Then, as if hypnotized, he looked in the direction of the saloon on the opposite side, noticed the group of men lounging there and the expression of fear on his face increased noticeably.

'Just keep moving slow and easy to the saloon,' the Kid ordered. 'I've had three mounts brought over from the livery stables for you.'

'This might prove to be the last murder you commit, outlaw,' snapped Stratford harshly, turning his head and staring directly at the Kid, lips thin.

'This sheriff here ain't no fool, I guess. He'll soon set this matter to rights and then he'll be on to your trail so fast, you won't have a chance.'

The Kid moved forward with the silence and stealth of a panther. His bunched fist caught the other on the side of the head, knocking him sideways, off balance. Stratford fell back against one of the wooden uprights, spitting blood. He crouched, made to move in against the other, stopped dead in his tracks as the Kid snapped: 'Don't try it, Stratford! There'll be a dozen slugs in you before you can move. We're takin' you three out of town for a little pow-wow.'

Stratford sucked in a harsh breath. He stared wildly at the two other men with him. His hair had fallen over his eyes when the Kid had hit him and he thrust it away with an abrupt movement of his right hand.

'They're not taking us for any talk,' he said fiercely. 'They mean to kill us because we know too much. We saw the face of one of them.' He pointed across the street to the saloon, 'That killer there.' He motioned to Fleck. 'And now we've seen the whole bunch. They can't afford to let us live.'

The Kid looked past Stratford, lips tightened into a hard line. Then he said to Levin. 'Get them on to their mounts. If they make any kind of struggle, tie their hands to the saddlehorns.'

'If you intend to kill us then you'd better do it here, in full view of the town,' snapped Finney. 'You can all go to hell.'

There was an abrupt change in the atmosphere. Around them, the heat haze shimmered along the length of the street. Already, the men from the saloon had stepped down from the boardwalk and two of them were leading the three horses forward for the men standing in the middle of the street.

Finney's hard stare did not waver. He thrust his hands into his pockets, began to turn, to move back off the street. He had half turned when the Kid reversed his gun and brought the butt down hard on the side of Finney's head. The man crumpled at the knees without a sound, almost fell, then hung weakly as Levin and Gambel caught him by the arms and dragged him over to one of the horses.

'Throw him over the saddle and lash him down,' the Kid ordered. He kept a wary eye on the street but

although there were a few loafers around they seemed to
be taking no interest in what was going on. The Kid knew
their type. They did not interfere in anything which did
not concern them, had long since learned that a man lived
longer by keeping his nose clean.

Turning to Stratford and Meekin, he snapped. 'Get up
into the saddles. I'm tellin' you both for the last time.
Mount up!'

Stratford paused but Meekin was already hauling
himself up into the saddle, his face a mask of terror. After
a moment, Stratford's glance fell and he did likewise.

'Now you're showin' sense,' muttered the Kid. He
thrust the Colt back into leather, turned to take his own
mount.

A few curious stares followed them as they rode out of
Vendado, turned a bend in the trail and left the town
behind them. Two miles along the trail, they reined up.
Here was a rocky stretch of ground, some of the roughest
country in the territory around Vendado.

Calton looked across at the Kid, cocked an eye towards
the three men. 'This where you mean to finish 'em?' he
asked.

The Matagorda Kid sat without moving for a long
moment, his gaze sweeping over the three witnesses, then
he nodded. 'Sure. I reckon it's as good a place as any for
what we have to do. Take a look at Finney. He should be
comin' round about now. I want him to know why he's
bein' blasted into eternity.'

Haig Calton swung down, walked over to the man lying
across the saddle of the bay, grabbed him by the hair and
jerked his head back abruptly, staring into the man's face.
A faint groan came from the other and his eyes flicked
open, staring up at the sun as Calton held his head back
cruelly. For a moment, there was no sign of recognition in
his eyes, then memory came flooding back, he tried to
twist his head out of the other's grasp, but failed, sucked
air into his mouth as pain lanced through his head.

'All right, that's enough,' the Kid said. 'Get them off their horses and tie their hands behind their backs.'

Handling the men roughly, the outlaws dragged them from their mounts, cutting the thongs which bound their hands to the saddlehorns, and retied them behind them. Finney swayed on his feet as he faced the Kid. There was defiance still visible in his face as he swung his hot gaze around the circle of men around him. He balanced something briefly in his mind, then he said thinly: 'I wouldn't want to have what you're doing on my conscience. We wanted no part of this. We never wanted to see any of you men again. We'd have been away from Vendado, probably out of the territory by this time tomorrow and there would have been no danger to you.'

'We can't afford to take a chance like that,' the Kid said evenly, 'and you have only yourselves to blame for this. If you'd done as you were told on the train, and not tried to be a hero, this might never have happened.'

Meekin stood quite still, staring upward into the barrels of the guns that swung down to cover him. Perspiration dotted his upper lip, stained the front of his fancy shirt. Then, with a wild cry, he started forward, arms outstretched, fingers curled into talons, as he ran, uncaring, towards the Kid. He was almost at the Kid's mount, going flat on his heels for the final, forward leap. It was a foolish, crazy and fatal thing to do. A single shot rang out. It did not come from the gun held in the Kid's hand, although the barrel was levelled on the straining man and his finger was tightening on the trigger. Rather the shot that hit Meekin in the back as he tried to reach up for his tormentor's arm, came from the gun which Haig Calton had swung on him. The slug made a sickening, meaty sound as it tore into his body, and Meekin, knocked forward by the impact, struck the horse's flank as he went down, arms flailing helplessly. The horse shied away, whinneying shrilly and the Kid fought it down savagely, cursing under his breath.

Even as he did so, Finney and Stratford took this opportunity to make a run for it. It was a futile gesture. Their arms tied behind their backs, it was impossible to run fast, or to weave from side to side. There was a splash of flame from the Kid's Colt, another from Levin's and the two men stumbled as if they had been kicked in the back by a mule. Two hard, flat echoes raced over the rocky plain.

The Kid holstered his gun. He said sharply: 'Drag those bodies over here beside this one. Reckon we may as well lay them out decently.' His remark brought a loud guffaw from the men. Tense men were suddenly released from their tension. They spun this way and that on their horses while two men got down, hauled the dead men over to where Meekin lay face downward in the dirt. 'You goin' to waste time buryin' them?' inquired Calton thinly.

'Nope. We got no time for that. Those townsfolk back there may decide not to wait for the sheriff to return before comin' after us. Let's get back.'

They began moving away, gigging their horses along the rocky trail that swung north a couple of miles further on. There was a strangely exultant smile on the Kid's face as he sat forward in the saddle.

The bodies of the three men were found some hours later, a little before sundown, by Clem Roderick, one of the few prospectors still working the rivers in the hills. Roderick made a periodic visit into town every three months for supplies and on this particular day he had left the shack in the low foothills a little after dawn, making his way along trails known only to him and the Indians who had made them countless years before. Seated astride his bay, with the burro plodding contentedly behind, he scarcely looked up at all after reaching the main trail. As usual, he had seen no one all day and what with the heat and the alkali dust which had turned his mouth and throat into an oven, he felt weary as he rode, head nodding forward on to his chest, eyes lidding and closing.

Turning a bend in the trail, he felt the sudden slackening of his mount, jerked himself upright in the saddle, screwing up his eyes in an attempt to ascertain what it was that had scared his horse. At first he could see nothing. The red glare of the sun was shining directly into his eyes, making it hard to see anything properly.

'What's wrong, fella,' he said hoarsely. 'Easy now. Ain't nothin' here to be a-sceered of.'

The horse halted, then moved forward a dozen uncertain paces, feet shuffling in the dirt, head lowered a little. Peering into the red haze, Roderick noticed something lying in the tangled brush that grew alongside the trail a couple of yards ahead. Stiffly, he got down from the saddle, went forward cautiously, his hand close to the ancient pistol he carried at his waist. His breath caught up, rasping harshly in his throat as he bent over the inert, crumpled body. He stood there, bent slightly forward with his eyes popped wide and mouth hanging slackly open. 'Hellfire,' he murmured softly to himself.

For perhaps the space of a dozen heartbeats, he remained there, then he straightened up and turned stiffly to make his way back to the horse. As he did so, he threw a quick glance further along the trail, saw the other two bodies which lay close by and the blood drained from his face as he examined them closely. All had their hands tied behind their backs and there were bullet holes in their backs.

'I'd better git the sheriff,' he murmured to himself. The bodies were cold, had obviously been dead for some little time and it was clear there was nothing he could do for them. Hauling himself up into the saddle, he kicked spurs against the horse's flanks, forced it into a swift canter until he came within sight of Vendado. Once he entered the main street, he slowed a little. He had intended going straight to the saloon, to wash the trail dust from his throat, but what he had found on the trail had put that idea clear out of his mind. He did not rein up his mount until he came to the sheriff's office. A yellow light showed through the window and there was a thin strip of light under the door.

Clint McCorg had arrived back in town less than half an hour before. It had been a long ride from the hills and they had pushed their mounts hard. The fact that the outlaw band had not been at the cabin in the hills when they had found it and had not shown up while they had been there, had worried him more than he wanted to admit, even to himself. The outlaw gang was somewhere on the loose and God alone knew what devilry they were committing. He had expected to find trouble in Vendado when he had ridden back with the posse, Menderer carrying the body of the dead outlaw across his saddle, but the town had seemed quiet enough and once he had put up his mount at the livery stable, he had washed the trail dust out of his throat and then come back here to the office, to rest his saddle-weary body and try to think things out logically in his mind.

At this point, the door opened and Clem Roderick came in, stood blinking owlishly in the light for a moment, then closed the door and shuffled forward.

McCorg sighed. 'What's on your mind, Clem,' he asked. 'You look like you've just seen a ghost.'

'I seen three of 'em, Sheriff,' muttered the other. He stepped up to the edge of the desk. 'I don't reckon you've got a bottle anywhere around, have you?'

The other stared at him for a moment, then opened a drawer in the desk and took out the whiskey bottle. The other snatched at it greedily, drank thirstily and noisily from it before setting it down on the desk, and wiping his lips with the back of his hand.

'Thanks, Sheriff. I sure needed that.'

'All right, Clem. Now suppose you tell me what happened.' He let his cool stare fall on the other's grizzled features.

'There's three dead men lyin' by the side of the trail,

less than a couple of miles out of town, Sheriff. They been shot in the back by the looks of 'em.'

McCorg sucked in a deep breath through tightly clenched teeth. 'You know any of them?' he asked, after he had digested the full import of what the other had said.

'Nope. Not a one, Sheriff. But it sure looked to me as if somebody had been havin' themselves a time. They was city gents too, by their clothes.'

McCorg felt a little twinge of apprehension go through him. Something clicked into place in his mind. With a sudden movement, he thrust back his chair, got to his feet and moved around the edge of the desk. 'I'm goin' to check on somethin', Clem,' he said harshly. There was a note of cold authority in his tone. 'I shall want you to take me back to where these bodies are in fifteen minutes. Where'll I find you?'

The other shrugged. 'Reckon I'll get myself a bite to eat at Chinese Charley's. I'll be there when you want me, Sheriff.'

McCorg nodded. He followed the other out into the street, closed the office door. While Roderick made his way to the restaurant, McCorg walked quickly to the hotel. There was nobody behind the desk as he went into the lobby but a moment later, the door of the dining-room opened and a weedy looking individual came in. His brows lifted a little as he recognized the other.

'Howdy, Sheriff. Something I can do for you?'

'I reckon so. You've got three men stayin' here, names of Finney, Meekin and Stratford.'

'That's right.' The other nodded emphatically.

'Can I see them? It's important.'

'I'm afraid they aren't here, Sheriff,' said the other apologetically. 'I understand they left this morning some-time and so far they haven't returned.'

'You know if they left together, or if there was anybody with them?'

The clerk pursed his lips, shook his head. 'I couldn't

say. I wasn't on duty then. But Agnew can help you. You'll find him in the dining-room, just inside the door. He was here this morning.'

'Thanks.' McCorg went into the dining room, glanced about him for a moment, then spotted the small figure of the man who sat alone at the nearest table. He walked over to him, pulled back the other chair at the table and lowered himself wearily into it. The other glanced up in sudden surprise, then relaxed as he saw who it was.

'Mind if I ask you a few questions, Agnew?'

The other hesitated, then shrugged. 'Not at all, Sheriff. If I can answer them, I will.'

'Those three city gents who came in on the train that was held up. They were stayin' here for a few days, I understand.'

'That's right.' There was a faint look of perplexity on the clerk's face. 'But I'm afraid I don't understand. Have they done anything against the law?'

'Nope. But I've just had a report from some prospector who's just ridden in with word that he found three bodies along the trail, a couple of miles away, and from the descriptions he gave, it sounds like those three men.'

'But why should anyone want to—' The other broke off as a fresh thought struck him. He went on quickly, excitedly: 'Those men who came in this morning and went out with them. But why would they kill them?'

'Would you know these men again if you saw them?'

'I think so,' mused the other. He nodded his head. 'I'm sure I would,' he continued. 'Say, was that the same gang that held up the train?'

'Could have been,' McCorg conceded. 'If I'm right, you can consider yourself a very fortunate man.'

'That they didn't shoot me?'

'That's right.'

'They also the same bunch you and the posse rode out for?' The other's shrewd eyes had seen a lot of living in this town and there wasn't any doubting the implication behind that statement.

'I guess so. We brought back one of them across a saddle, but there was no sign of the others up in their hide-out, or of the money they took from the train. I reckon they must've hidden it someplace else in the hills.'

He got to his feet, pushed back the chair. 'Thanks for the information, Agnew,' he said.

He located Roderick in Chinese Charley's restaurant. The other was just finishing his meal. He gave McCorg a sharp-bright stare. 'You figure you know who those *hombres* might be, Sheriff?'

McCorg nodded, seated himself at the table and eyed the other closely. Roderick was a wizened old man of indeterminate age, his jacket and shirt almost black with grease and dirt. His face was brown and wrinkled, like a walnut, his beard a tangled mass of brown and grey. Only the eyes that stared out at McCorg seemed to have something of life and youth in them. He took a corncob pipe from his pocket, a pouch from the other, gazed into it soulfully for a moment, then folded it up and put it back, a sorrowful look on his face.

McCorg grinned. 'Here, old-timer,' he said, extending his own pouch. 'Take a fill of this, then we'll head out to where you located these bodies.'

'Thanks, Sheriff.' The other stuffed the strands of tobacco into the bowl of the pipe, waited until he had it going, then sat forward in his chair. 'Now, what d'you want to know?'

McCorg shrugged. 'Reckon there ain't much you can tell me,' he said easily. 'Those men could be three *hombres* who put up at the hotel a couple of days ago. One of 'em unmasked a member of the gang that did the robbery and all three got a good look at him. I figure the gang decided to silence them all permanently rather than run the risk of ever being identified.'

'Reckon they made a good job of it then, Sheriff.' The

other lifted the glass of whiskey from the table. He held it in his hand for a moment, then a hole appeared in his beard and he tossed the liquor down with a single gulp.

By the time they rode out of town it was full dark. The moon had not yet risen and there were a few ridges of cloud hiding the stars to the north and east. The wind blew uncommonly cold for the time of year and McCorg pulled up the collar of his jacket as they hit the long, sweeping ridge, devoid of tree or vegetation. As they climbed higher, the night wind, chilled by the elevation, struck at them with an almost icy touch. Then they reached a flat, set their horses at a steady canter. Even though it was so dark, Roderick led the way with confidence and any doubts that McCorg may have had as to the truth of what the other had told him were lost quickly. They were still high up and there was the feeling of high mountains tilted against them, tall peaks on their left, and ten miles or more of grassy, flat ground to their right, a darkly shimmering mass in the pale stargleam.

Roderick reined up suddenly, sat the saddle for a moment looking about him. 'I reckon it was about here I found 'em,' he murmured. 'Guess we'd better go slow now.'

'We'll get down and lead the horses,' McCorg said. He did not relish wasting much time in the cold darkness searching for three dead men.

They drifted forward slowly, eyes searching on all sides of them. Against the rim of the ridge which here ran parallel with the trail, he made out the gaunt stumps of stunted trees, blown into fantastic shapes by the continual wind which seemed to become funnelled here, sweeping endlessly between desert and mountain.

'You sure this is the place?' he muttered sharply after several minutes of tiring, fruitless searching.

'Almost sure, Sheriff.' The other did not sound quite as confident now as he had earlier. 'But in the dark, every place looks nearly alike and—' He broke off suddenly, moved off the trail into the rough ground to one side. 'Here, Sheriff,' he called. 'Here's one of 'em. The others will be close by.'

McCorg went forward, bent beside the crumpled body that lay alongside the trail, turned it over and struck a match. In the brief yellow flare, he looked down at the man's face, sucked in a sharp hiss of air. 'This is Finney all right,' he muttered, half to himself. 'Shot in the back like you said.' His lips were stretched thin across his face. 'We'd better get them into town. Too many coyotes out here.'

Together, they lifted the men across their saddles, tied them down, then began the long walk back to Vendado.

The inquest on the three men took place in the back room of the hotel in Vendado the following morning, a back room which had been specially cleared for the purpose. Carew, the banker acted as coroner.

To McCorg, watching from the back of the room, it was obvious that the other had never been called upon to do this particular chore before and he was uncertain of what to do. Nevertheless, he had dressed himself up in long black frock coat and had assumed some kind of dignity in spite of his unassuming appearance.

Rapping on the low table, he opened the proceedings: 'Now this won't be a long, drawn-out affair,' he said fussily. 'Far as I can see, there isn't much we can do here, except confirm the cause of death and—'

He paused at an outbreak of laughter from the citizens in the front row of the audience. One of the men yelled: 'Since they was all shot in the back, Carew, reckon we don't need you to tell us they was murdered.'

'Quiet!' shouted the banker. 'I'm here to see that this inquest is carried through legally and properly.'

McCorg eyed the other more closely. Carew had a lean and kindly face, the silvery hair shining a little in the sunlight which flooded the room. He coughed and fussed as he examined the papers in front of him, possibly not understanding any of them, but trying to look the part which had been forced upon him by circumstance. Most of the time, he merely succeeded in giving a theatrical appearance as he sat stiff-backed in the chair facing everyone.

'I'm going to call the witnesses now,' he said evenly. 'First of all I want Eli Telfer, to tell us what he saw on the morning in question.'

The clerk from the hotel rose a little sheepishly from his chair, advanced to the front of the room and gave his evidence a trifle hesitantly. He seemed self-possessed, but nervous. Making his deposition, he told how the group of riders had entered the hotel, asked for the room number of Finney's apartment and had then gone upstairs, coming down a while later – he wasn't sure how much later as he had not taken too much notice of them – with the three guests. How they had left with the riders, saying that they might be away for a while, but would be back in time for the evening meal. That was the last time he had seen any of the men, until he had been taken by the sheriff to identify the bodies in the town mortuary.

Clem Roderick told how he had stumbled across the three bodies on his way down from the hills, how he had notified the sheriff and they had gone out together after dark the previous evening to bring them in. Carew questioned him closely as to whether he had noticed any group of riders during the afternoon along the trail, but Roderick had seen no one.

Finally, McCorg was called to give evidence. He gave his evidence precisely, confirming most of Roderick's story. In the darkness, it had been impossible to make out any tracks, although since this was the main trail to the north, it was doubtful if they would be able to tell anything from a study of the tracks. The bodies had been found among the scrub which bordered the trail and although there were signs that two of them had been shot while they were running and their bodies dragged some distance to the point where they had been found, there was little else to indicate what had happened.

When he had finished his evidence, Carew cleared his throat noisily, turned to address the jury. He was diffident in his manner, several times stopping himself as he tried to find the right legal term to express what he had in mind, and sometimes suffering an acute embarrassment as laughter rose from the crowd in the small room.

Watching his flushed features, McCorg guessed how the other felt. This was the first time there had been a murder like this around Vendado since he had been sheriff and it did not often happen that they had to hold an inquest such as this. Any shooting in the town was usually between two men who each held a gun, and a verdict was seldom needed. The victim was buried up on Boot Hill and the incident forgotten. But they could not forget or overlook this cold-blooded murder, and he knew that the full weight of bringing the killers to justice rested with him.

Carew finished his short speech, summed up the evidence as best he could in the circumstances, then indicated that the jury might have time in which to think over their verdict if they wished. The whole proceedings were casual and sometimes sadly lacking in order, but it did not take long for the jury to make up its mind. The verdict was that the three men had been kidnapped from their hotel, taken at gunpoint out of town and there ruthlessly murdered to prevent them from talking. The murderers were members of the same outlaw band which had blown up the railroad and robbed the incoming train from Tucson.

The fact that only one of the outlaws had been killed did not bother them in the least. They had done their part by bringing in this verdict of murder. It was now the duty of the sheriff to bring these men to justice.

FOUR
Outlaw

Slowly, the hours went by on crawling feet. The sun climbed steeply to its zenith and the heat haze hung over Vendado until the outlines of the buildings shivered in the harsh white glare and every breath a man took was a torture in his lungs. Clint McCorg waited while the heat head diminished, waited until the flaring disc of the sun began its swifter horizonward drop, then got up from the chair on which he had been sitting outside the jailhouse in the shade of the wooden overhang, stretched himself, and walked over to the livery stables. The groom saw him coming and drifted out of the back, eyeing him curiously.

'You headin' out after them varmints what killed those three men, Sheriff?' he inquired hopefully, teetering on one foot for a moment. 'Could be that the scent will be pretty cold by now.'

'Could be,' said the other non-committally. 'Reckon though there ain't nothin' to be found here in town.'

The other brought him his mount, watched patiently while McCorg checked the cinch, tightening it a little under the horse's belly. Then he stepped up into the saddle. Glancing down, he saw the other watching him with a faint expression of surprise on his features. 'You ain't thinkin' of ridin' out after that bunch alone, are you?'

McCorg shrugged. 'We located their hide-out yesterday. I'm figurin' that when they get back and find their lookout was killed, they'll either decide to make a run for it to the border, or hunt around for another hide-out. If they head across the border, ain't nothin' I can do. My jurisdiction don't extend that far, but if they're figurin' on sticking around here for a while yet, then the sooner I know about that, the better.'

'Still don't make no sense goin' out after them alone. You can't have a hope in hell of takin' the whole bunch.'

McCorg smiled thinly. 'I wasn't aimin' to do that,' he told the other. 'I'm just wantin' to find their freshest trail right now. And a bunch of riders would be spotted ten miles away in that hill country whereas one man could slip through without bein' noticed.'

The other gave an odd chuckle, part wise and part foolish. 'Hope you know what you're doin', Sheriff,' was his parting remark. There was a look of sly humour on his face as he nodded, then stepped back into the long shadows inside the stables.

McCorg rode slowly along the shadowed street, stopped halfway along it to give his mount a drink from the long trough, then continued on until he was out of town when he gave the horse its head. The rattle of its hooves on the stony underfooting of the road was the only sound to break the stillness and this died away quickly in the stunted timber skirting the trail. He rode quickly, eyes on the trail in front of him, looking for sign. There were the marks of many horses, making it virtually impossible to pick out anything which would help him.

To his right, across the stretching plains, the tall grass shimmered and rippled in long, sweeping waves where the wind bent it, until far off, even these movements faded in the hazy immensity towards the horizon. McCorg doubted if the outlaws would ride back to check on whether the bodies of the men they had slain had been discovered. By now, he reckoned, they were miles away, probably planning their next move.

Glumly, his mind ran over the events of the past few days and he wondered where he could even start looking for these outlaw killers. Before, when they had held up a stage, they had been content with taking what gold and valuables they could lay their hands on, but now that they had added cold-blooded murder to their crimes, it was a little too much to expect that they would hesitate to kill again whenever it suited them. These men were like prairie wolves; whenever they got the taste of blood, it stayed with them, something which could never be washed off.

Even thinking of this brought back painful memories to him and he tried to push the thought out of his mind, concentrating on watching the trail. As he rode, he recognized certain landmarks from the previous evening's ride with the old prospector, and at last, he came to the spot where they had found the three slain men. Dismounting, he searched the area thoroughly. Here and there, in the shifting dust, he found footmarks which he soon satisfied himself were those of the two men who had tried to run when they saw death staring at them out of the round, black muzzles of levelled guns. The marks made when the two bodies had been dragged over the ground were also clearly visible, but as for the rest — There were confused hoofmarks from which he could gain no information. Baffled, he began to search further afield, moving in wider circles from the place where the bodies had lain.

He doubted if the killers would have stayed long on the trail. Sooner or later, they would have pulled away from it, headed either up into the hills or down across the prairie. Where were they now and why had they not shot these men on the train when they had had a far better opportunity? It had taken a lot of nerve to ride straight into Vendado, kidnap these three men from the hotel in broad daylight, ride them out here and shoot them down in this seemingly senseless manner. Yet there had to be an answer to it somewhere. Had it been a sudden change of heart, the realization that no longer would they be able to ride into a town quite openly, pick up whatever information they could and then ride on out again to plan their robbery? That sounded likely. The questions plagued him endlessly, buzzing round and round inside his brain like a cloud of humming mosquitoes, hammering at him with an infuriating vexation which he found difficult to control. There had been talk in Vendado, just after the robbery that a group of men had been seen haunting the saloons and stores in Tucson, that they had also been seen riding out just before dawn on the day that the train had been held up. Things began to tie in a little, but there were still several aspects of this case that puzzled him.

He straightened up with an audible grunt, rubbed the muscles at the nape of his neck. There was still that deepseated weariness in him and he realized that it was some days now since he had last had a good night's sleep. Slowly, he pivoted on the spot where he stood, casting about him, then narrowed his eyes as he noticed the faint trail that led through the bending grass. It was little more than a narrow line where the grass had been crushed underfoot, the stalks bruised and darkened.

This had been done quite recently, he mused. Lifting his head, he stared off towards the horizon. It was just possible that anyone riding in that direction could swing sharply and enter the range of hills where he knew the outlaws to have their hide-out, from the east. It was a circuitous, longer route than one through the rocks, but it was just the sort of thing these outlaws might do to throw him off the trail. Squinting up at the westering sun, he gauged there to be another four or five hours of daylight left. His best bet was to take that trail and follow it as far as he could, see whether his suspicions were right. Swinging easily into the saddle, he pulled the horse off the trail, rode out into the grass. The going was easy here and this, he reflected, may also have swayed the outlaws into taking this trail, rather than climbing the rocks.

He hit the lower reaches of a creek an hour later, kept to its winding bank for the best part of a mile, then plunged into a thickly tangled grove of trees and brush. By degrees, the country had changed. As he had anticipated, the trail led him into the rough country to the east of the hills, the ground beginning to rise slowly now. Far off to his left, he heard harsh bawling from a herd of cattle, made to ride on by, then reined up as the thought came to him that the men herding the cows may have seen something the previous day. Knowing his usual run of luck, he thought bitterly, it was hardly likely, but at the moment, he had no clues at all and anything, any piece of information, no matter how small and seemingly insignificant, would be a godsend.

As he waited, a stream of steers poured over the skyline in a ragged wave, filing down towards the creek. There were some riders accompanying them and one signalled to him as they came nearer.

'Howdy, Sheriff,' said the other quietly. Grey eyes watched McCorg directly, but without suspicion. 'Lookin' for someone?'

'That's right,' McCorg nodded. 'Could be you can help me. Bunch of outlaws kidnapped three men from Vendado yesterday, shot 'em down in cold blood along the trail back yonder. I judged their trail led this way and was wonderin' if you or any of your boys saw anythin' of them yesterday.'

'A small outfit did ride through,' nodded the other. 'Stopped for a bite and coffee to wash the trail dust from their throats, then moved on, said they was mighty anxious to get to Tucson before dark. Don't see how they'd make it, but they lit out of camp in an all-fired hurry after they'd eaten.'

'Sounds like the bunch I'm lookin' for,' conceded McCorg. He glanced musingly in the direction of the hills which loomed on the nearby horizon. 'But once they get up there, it'll take an army to find 'em. Too many trails twistin' through there. Too many places where men can hide.'

'Guess you're right at that.' The other scratched his cheek reflectively. 'But one of those men was ridin' a lame horse. Asked if we had one we could sell him, but we don't have any spare horseflesh here at the line camp. My guess is he wouldn't get far on that mount.'

'Doubt if that would slow 'em up much.'

'Heard one of them say that if this *hombre* couldn't keep up with them they'd move on without him.'

McCorg lifted his brows a little at that. If it were true, it could mean that the outlaws were more jittery than he had thought, wanted to put as much distance between themselves and any likely pursuit as possible, even to the extent of leaving behind one of their number to run the risk of being taken prisoner, rather than slow themselves up for a lame horse.

'We'll be makin' camp soon, Sheriff,' went on the other. 'If you'd care to wait awhile, you're welcome to some vittles.'

'Thanks, but I figure I'd better be ridin' on. Could be that *hombre* with the lame mount didn't get too far after all and I may be able to track him in the hills.'

'Well, I sure wish you luck, Sheriff,' said the other, raising his right hand in salute. 'But they seemed a tough bunch of men to me. You wouldn't have much of a chance if you bumped into the whole bunch of 'em.'

Splashing over a wide stream, McCorg rode upgrade into the foothills, following the tracks which were still just visible. Branches had been snapped off the trees and bushes which lined the trail and it was obvious that the outlaws had not been cautious, had probably figured they had thrown any pursuers off their trail long before they reached this point. Slanting up through the timber that covered the lower slopes, he presently came to a huge wrinkle in the ground where an ancient slide had opened a smooth channel in the rock face. The track led right up to the natural chute and here, he could plainly make out the tracks of the horses. He rode carefully up the chute, sitting well back in the saddle to give his mount balance. In places, the gradient was so steep that it was all he could do to keep the horse moving. Every step it took threatened to send it sliding back to the bottom. But in the end, he reached the level stretch of smooth rock and paused there to look behind him. Above the slanted branches of the trees, he could just make out the flatness of the prairie and far below him, little more than tiny-seeming black dots, the cattle and the riders who herded them around the bank of the creek.

Daylight was beginning to fade on this side of the hills. The sun, dipping down to the west, was completely hidden by the upper summits and the trail lay in shadow about him. Here, the country was a little more open than previously, rising and falling in a series of undulating swells, dotted here and there by patches of brush and clumps of twisted, gnarled trees. He gave his mount its head, letting it run hard in the coolness that came flowing down from the tops of the hills.

In the cool grey dimness of evening, he reached the place where the outlaws had made camp. They had built a fire here, rested up for the night and then ridden on sometime that morning. There was a small stream nearby that ran swiftly over the rocks, bubbling and foaming in its headlong rush down the steep hillside. This was where they would make camp, he thought, getting down from the saddle, and examining the area closely. Next to water, and it was just possible that it would be here that any decision would be taken about the rider with the lame mount. If they had any sense, they would let him ride on, through the night, ahead of them, while they made camp. That way, they would catch up with him sometime during the morning, and nothing would have been lost. On the other hand, he reflected grimly, since he and the posse had not found that gold and paper currency anywhere around their hide-out, it meant they had hidden it somewhere deeper in the hills and it was unlikely there would be sufficient trust among them to allow one man to go riding on ahead of them. That way, he might grab off all of the gold for himself and be over the border before they caught up with him again.

He moved his horse forward to the stream, let it drink while he examined the prints along the bank. Five minutes later, he found what he had been looking for, The tracks of a solitary rider, moving away from the main bunch. From the depths of the hoofprints, where they were clearly visible in patches of soft earth, it was easy to see that this was the lame horse in the bunch. Vaguely, he wondered who the man was who rode this particular mount, Certainly not the leader of the outlaws, he would undoubtedly have the best mount for himself. But if it was the man who had pulled the trigger which had sent even one of those three men into eternity . . .

Rolling himself a smoke, he lit it, smoked in reflective silence for a while, then climbed wearily back into the saddle. He looked at the shadows around him and thought: He could be miles away by now, yet there is the chance he can be only a short distance away, especially if his mount had gone really lame on him.

It grew darker as he progressed along the winding trail and after a time, he found it more and more difficult to ensure he was on the right track. Presently, however, it led him into the upper reaches of the hills at the eastern end of the range. At this point, his quarry had turned aside from the trail, moving into the tall, first-growth pine, massive at the butt and then rising in a flawless, sweeping line towards the blue-purple heavens. Here, sheltered by the trees from anyone who might be watching the trail, he gave his horse chance to blow before continuing on. In the cool silence that lay over the hills, he could hear the

faint chittering of a squirrel among the lower branches
and the more distant sound of birds. It would be only a
matter of time before he had followed this trail all the way
across the hills, right to the point where he and the posse
had discovered the outlaws' hideaway. If he did not
succeed in catching up with his quarry before then, there
would be little point in going on. He would need men at
his back before he tackled the whole gang.

He knew none of this particular stretch of land, yet he
felt no inward concern. All his life, he had been close to
the land, had known the stretching distances of the prairie
and the alkali dust deserts, the varied pattern of hill and
river, the cold dark limits of the night and the hot sunglare
of the day. His home had been wherever the night had
found him, beside the gleam of a camp-fire, sometimes on
a ranch, lately in Vendado. Never, in the whole of his life
had there been the need for anything more than this,
except whenever he thought of Mary. Only then, were
there times when it seemed as if there might be something
more to life than riding the different trails which opened
up before a man.

He edged his mount forward through the tangled
thorn that grew in profusion around the trunks of the
pine. He was almost out of the timberwood, when he
heard the faint, far-off echo that hung on the breeze for a
few seconds before fading into extinction. Riding, he
listened for it to be repeated, but there was no further
sound. In the blue-shadowed world that lay all about him,
he searched the dimness, pushing his sight through the
breaks in the trees. When he did finally come out into the
open, the rocks that jutted out from the sides of the trail
where it ran down through a cleft in the steep-sided walls,
were sharply etched against the skyline. The ground was
cold and there was a clinging dampness in the air that
clearly came from some river running off to his left at the
bottom of the steep drop that fell away into darkness.
Pausing, he picked out the murmur of water rushing over

stones far below. He had been riding forward, slowly, a little surer of himself. Then, without warning, a rifle shot blasted out of the silence, the bullet struck the rock within a foot of him, the lead screaming into the distance with the shrill bleat of tortured metal. The horse whinnied, swung away from the rocky wall on their right. McCorg had been holding on lightly to the reins. Now, with this sudden, frightened movement on the part of his mount, he fell sideways in the saddle, arms flailing madly. As he lost his balance, his grip tightened spasmodically on the reins and as he fell sideways, one foot still taut in the stirrups, he struggled to swing back, to come upright; at the same time, easing the horse back along the trail. A second shot rang out, striking splinters of knife-edged rock out from the ledge immediately above him. Something sliced along his arm, raking the flesh as it tore through the sleeve of his jacket.

Wincing involuntarily, he threw himself out of the saddle, fell against the rocky wall of the chasm, whipped himself sharply around, drawing the Colt from its holster in a single striking movement. The horse, still alarmed, moved backward with him, half dragging him along the rough outcrops of rock that scraped his arms and legs, sawing at his ribs. With an effort, he got one elbow hooked over an outjutting rock, hung on for dear life, feeling a momentary sharp pain lancing through his chest. All of the air seemed to have been knocked out of his lungs, leaving him temporarily weak and helpless. Screwing up his eyes, he tried to probe the darkness around him, seeking the muzzle blast of the rifle, anything to give away the hiding place of the man who had tried to kill him. Inwardly, he was cursing himself for riding into an ambush with his eyes closed. Had he been careful and as attentive as he should have been, knowing that his quarry might not be too far ahead of him, he should have never put himself into a position where it would be possible for a killer to bushwhack him.

Feet digging against the wall of the canyon, he pushed himself on to his knees, still gripping the Colt tightly, Except for the skittering movements of his mount, no sound disturbed the utter stillness. He could hear the blood pounding through his head, the breath rasping in his throat. With an effort, he forced his heart into a slower, more normal, beat. His body had taken a bruising beating from that dragging along the rocks and several seconds passed before he was able to get into a half crouch and ease his way gently forward to where the rocky wall slanted downward, opening out at the canyon mouth into more open country.

He estimated that the dry-gulcher was crouched somewhere among the high rocks that overlooked the end of the canyon, sited in the best spot from which he could look along the canyon entrance and spot anything that moved. He drew a couple of deep breaths and felt relieved when no more shots came blasting down the natural funnel formed by the rocks. If the hidden gunman had his wits about him, he would send several shots ricocheting along the canyon, bouncing the leaden slugs off the walls that hemmed him in. That way he could keep McCorg pinned down without exposing himself and there would be a good chance that one of the ricocheting shots would hit him.

Bending low, he crawled along the narrow defile at the entrance of the canyon, keeping his head down, straining eyes and ears for the slightest movement and faintest sound, but whoever it was out there was not giving himself away. Reaching the end of the canyon, he lay flat on his stomach, lifted his head slightly and studied the terrain thoughtfully. He was, he reflected, a little lower than the gunman's position. To the left there was the sheer drop into the depths of the yawning chasm with the faint murmur of water splashing and bubbling at the bottom, perhaps two hundred feet down. To the right, was a pine-thick slope and dead ahead, the trail continued, narrowing a little until it wound around the side of a tall abutment and vanished from sight. Ten feet from where he lay, there was a steep slope that led up into the pines over-looking the trail. It could be climbed, he did not doubt that, but much of it was nothing more than bare rock and it would take time, and every second he was on that slope, he would be exposed to the hidden marksman.

He cast about him for some other way up the slope. At first, he could make out little in the deep shadows. Then, abruptly, almost before he was expecting it, he saw the sudden movement at the very edge of his vision, in the lower pines. He raised the Colt, aimed and fired in the same instant. Too late, the other was down behind one of the trees. Pressing himself in against the cold, hard rock, he waited, staring hard at the place where the other had disap-peared. Now he knew where the killer was. It was up to him whether he went in after him, or remained where he was and waited him out. All of this went through McCorg's mind and he concluded that so long as he had the other pinned down, things were evened up. He determined to wait the other out; to see how long the killer's nerve would last. The tree behind which the other had gone down, was isolated from the rest, standing out in front of them, with a stretch of perhaps ten feet across which the man would have to move if he wanted to slip back into the timber. Lifting the Colt, he loosed off four quick shots, bracketing the spot where the other lay hidden. That would be sufficient warn-ing to him that he was pinned down completely, that even the darkness would not help him now.

Thumbing fresh shells into the chambers of the Colt, he propped himself up on his elbows, staring off into the blackness, not keeping his gaze fixed on any one spot for any length of time, knowing this to be fatal when watching for movement in the dark. There was no sense in being careless or in underestimating this man.

Thick and tangible, the silence settled about the two men, separated by thirty feet of open ground, each waiting for the other to make a move, to make a mistake. McCorg sucked air deeply into his lungs as he lay there, scarcely moving. Better let the quietness go to work on the other, he told himself. This was, in all probability, something which could best be resolved by patience. If it was at all possible, he wanted to take the other in alive. It might be they could get him to talk, turn State's evidence in return for saving his life.

Smiling thinly to himself, he eased his body upright, sat with his shoulders against the rock. No doubt the other was scheming as to the best way of getting out of the jam in which he found himself. He may have guessed who it was trailing him. He may even decide eventually to give himself up. McCorg's grin broadened a little in the darkness. That was not likely. These outlaws were wanted on a variety of charges in half a dozen different states and somewhere, no doubt, some lawman wanted him on a charge of murder. He would not give up easily.

Time passed slowly. Off beyond the fringe of trees, an owl hooted, the low melancholy echoes atrophying slowly as they chased themselves among the swaying branches. McCorg shifted position as his body became cramped, but not once did he let his gaze wander from the tree behind which the killer lay crouched. Half an hour later the moon rose, flooded the terrain with a pale, cold radiance, McCorg waited just a little longer, then eased his long body forward into the midnight shadows. His groping fingers found a large, flat rock and, moving swiftly, he tossed it along the trail, heard it strike loudly about thirty feet from him. The shot came almost in the same instant and this time, he saw the splash of vivid orange flame. He smiled a little in the darkness, although there was still the tension building up inside him. The killer might be all right when it came to shooting down innocent men, or robbing a train, but he's no good at this kind of job, he thought fiercely. He crept forward again, knowing that the other would be peering along the trail, suspecting that he had moved during the hour that had passed.

Seconds later, he heard the scrape of a boot on rock. It was followed a moment afterwards, by the metallic jingle made by the barrel of a rifle as it struck some projecting stone. The other was trying to pull out and in his hurry he had become careless and given himself and his intentions away.

Moving more quickly now, knowing that if the killer succeeded in getting into the timber, the chances were that he would lose him, McCorg reached the bottom of the slope which led upwards, crawled up it as quickly as he could. He made little noise, was almost at the top when he caught the sharp hiss of breath being sucked in through clenched teeth. The need for air had given the other's position away. Thumbing back the hammer, he fired at the sound, heard the slug tear bark and wood from the trunk of the trees, saw the dark shape that rose up, turned on its heel, and began to run for the trees.

'Hold it right there!' he called sharply. The words echoed loud in the narrowness and the man in front of him made his decision. McCorg saw him wheel swiftly, fling himself forward, legs churning in the loose shale and rock, turning to loose off a shot behind him as he ran. The bullet struck wide of his position and in the same instant, he fired. He had deliberately aimed low, saw the man stagger as the slug hit him in the leg. Then he went down, dropping the rifle, clawing at his thigh, trying to drag himself the rest of the way into the trees.

McCorg reached him a moment later, kicked the rifle into the brush, bent and pulled the two Colts from their holsters, thrusting them into his waist band.

'Goddamnit! You busted my leg with that shot.' The other ground the words out between his teeth. 'I'm in bad shape.'

'Guess you ought to be thankful I didn't aim to kill you,' McCorg snapped thinly. 'I'm thinkin' of those three innocent men you killed.'

Even in the shadowy darkness, he noticed the gust of

expression that went over the other's face at that, saw the man's lips slacken a little.

'I don't know what the hell you're talkin' about,' he growled. 'You've crippled me with that slug. Are you just goin' to squat there and do nothin' about it?'

'I'll dig it out when I'm good and ready,' McCorg said. 'At the moment, I want the answers to some questions and I reckon you're goin' to give 'em to me.'

'I don't know a damn thing.' The other lay back with a groan. His hands were on his chest, fingers tight, curled into hard fists.

'We'll see about that.' McCorg got to his feet, walked a few yards off. Behind him, the other suddenly called out in a high, anxious tone: 'You ain't goin' to leave me here, are you?'

McCorg swung on him, stared down at the injured man for a long moment without a word, then moved further into the brush, hunting for dry tinder. He guessed that the rest of the outlaws were far away by this time and it would be safe enough to light a fire. For a moment, as he collected twigs and brush, he felt a deep surge of anger rise within him and he almost regretted that he had aimed low. A little higher and this part of it would have been all over by now. Even though he held the whip hand over the other, there was the chance that he might not talk, or that whatever information he did give, might be lies.

He made out the scrape of the other's body as he shifted position on the hard ground. The man let out a heavy grunt as his leg twisted under him and collapsed back on to the rock with a faintly muffled cry of pain.

'You'd better lie still until I get a fire goin' and get that lead out of your leg,' he said thinly. 'Then I'm takin' you back to Vendado.'

'You won't get me very far,' said the other with a growing confidence. 'You forget that I'm not the only one. The Matagorda Kid will have me out of that jail before you know it.'

'I wouldn't bank on that if I were you.' McCorg built up the fire, watched the flames catch at the dry wood. Sparks lifted in a shower of red high into the air. Once the flames had a firm hold, he tossed a couple of handfuls of wood into the blaze, then went over to where the other lay. The bullet had smashed into the back of the other's thigh, five or six inches above the knee, burning through the flesh and lodging somewhere near the bone. The other would be lame, even when the slug was out and the wound had healed. He grinned a little to himself at the thought. Being lame was not going to bother this man none. Once he had been tried, he would end swinging at the end of a rope.

'This ain't goin' to be easy,' he muttered after examining the injury. 'The slug is still in there. I shall have to probe for it.'

'You goin' to fish for it now?' The other's tone was suddenly high pitched, afraid. His face was sharp and set as he stared up at McCorg.

'You got any other idea? That lead has got to come out.'

The other began groaning steadily as McCorg took out his knife, tested the blade with the ball of his thumb, then cut the cloth away from the wound, exposing the pale flesh. The outlaw twisted on the ground. 'Let the goddamned thing stay where it is,' he muttered thickly, his lips scarcely moving.

McCorg ignored his protestations. Whistling up his mount, he took down his canteen, washed most of the blood away from the wound. It was not as deep as he had anticipated. The angle of the shot had been such that it had entered obliquely, driving up into the flesh. Placing his knife on a stone so that the blade lay in the flames, he waited until it was red hot, then allowed it to cool.

All the time, he was aware of the man's eyes watching his every movement, of the pale sheen of them in the moonlight that filtered down through the trees close at hand. There was a dumb fear in the outlaw's eyes now, like that of an animal which had been hurt and lay waiting for the end.

'Pity we got no whiskey,' McCorg grunted. 'Might have helped the pain a little.'

The other drew in a hissing breath, teeth clenched tightly so that the muscle of his jaw lumped under the stubbled flesh. He kept turning on his shoulders, even before McCorg touched him, and his face was grey and bloodness, lips standing out darkly, forehead glistening damp with sweat. The pupils of his eyes seemed larger and darker than usual.

He squirmed as McCorg gripped his leg tightly with one hand, then inserted the blade of the knife into the ragged bullet hole. A great shudder passed through his body and he screamed thinly, head jerking from side to side. 'No, no!" he muttered under his breath. 'Leave it. Oh God, leave it alone.'

'I've got to clean this out.' McCorg felt a sense of disgust at the other. He had known men take a thing like this far better. He was not enjoying the other's pain, was simply used to it. A man did not ride these wide plains, these trails, without becoming something of a doctor, able to treat broken limbs and bullet wounds.

For a long moment, the other struggled frenziedly against him as the pain lanced through his body. Then his head fell back, striking the ground hard. His eyes were closed and a quick glance told McCorg that he had fainted. Well, perhaps it was better that way, he reflected. Now he could get on with the job. It took a long while. The bullet had sliced through the flesh and chipped the bone high up; but at last, the tip of the knife touched something hard and solid, that moved a little as he probed. Even then it took almost fifteen minutes to ease it out of the hole. Then it lay on the ground beside him, glistening redly in the pale moonlight. The man had not stirred. Wrapping the other's neckpiece around the wound to staunch the fresh bleeding, he got to his feet, went over to the fire and sat down beside it, feeling the warmth soak into his body. Even though the other was wounded, he did not trust him. Glancing up at the sky overhead, where the stars foamed into a yeasty ferment against the blackness, he knew it was going to be a long, weary night. There was no point in trying to retrace his steps now. Better to wait until dawn.

He rolled a cigarette, smoked it through slowly, trying to relax and think things out. Once, during the cold hours of the morning, the other stirred fitfully, groaned through his sleep, but did not waken. Watchfully, he waited for the first grey streaks of light to seep into the clearing.

He felt cold and hungry, stiff in his joints as he got up and tossed the last of the wood he had collected on to the fire. The glowing embers caught as he blew on them and when he straightened and turned, he saw that the other was stirring, struggling to sit up, pushing himself upward on his hands, his face grey and lined, lips drawn back into a snarl of effort. He sat for a long moment staring down at the neckpiece tied around his leg, then put out a hand gingerly and touched it, wincing a little as a stab of pain went through him.

He sat like that for several seconds, then looked up, as if seeing McCorg there for the first time.

'Did you get that lead out?' he asked. His voice was no more than a husky whisper.

'It's out,' McCorg said. He got up. 'You want somethin' to drink?'

The man nodded. He took the canteen and emptied it, tilting it up to his lips, the water dribbling down his chin.

'Got anythin' to eat?' The other rubbed the back of his hand across his lips as he spoke.

'Jerked beef and beans.' McCorg nodded towards the fire. Without moving, he went on: 'You know, you could maybe save yourself from the rope if you decided to talk. We know the Matagorda Kid planned that hold-up of the train, just as he did the stages that have been robbed. We want him more'n we want the little men who ride with him.' He eyed the other closely. 'I reckon I've seen your face on a poster someplace before.' Now that he could see the other's face clearly for the first time in the dawnlight, he sifted through the names and faces in his mind, then nodded briefly. 'I thought so. Ed Fleck. Wanted for armed robbery. I guess we can make that charge stick, if nothin' else.'

FIVE
The Angry Men

Clint McCorg rode into Vendado with his prisoner a little before noon the next day. Depositing him in one of the cells, he left Menderer on duty and went along to Chinese Charley's for a bite to eat. While he was there, Carew came inside, looked about him for a moment, spotted McCorg, and walked over to his table.

'Figured I might find you here, Sheriff,' he said easily. He seated himself in the other chair, laid his hat on the table in front of him. 'Saw you ride in while ago with one of those killers. Any idea who he is?'

'Name's Fleck. I've got a notice about him in my desk. Armed robbery with violence in Missouri and Texas.'

'And you're sure he's tied in with these killers?'

'Positive.' McCorg pushed the meat stew on to his fork with a piece of bread and chewed it thoughtfully. His stomach growled contentedly. 'His horse had gone lame on him and the others had ridden on ahead, probably expectin' him to catch up with 'em. When he doesn't, they may try to find out what happened to him. Or they may decide that there's one less to split the money with, share out their loot, and then ride for the border.'

Carew considered that for a moment, then shrugged; 'I've been givin' this whole matter a great deal of thought since the inquest,' he said slowly. 'I doubt if they'll head

for the border. This seems to be the kind of frontier territory they like, good pickings to be had, and the nearest
Army post more'n two hundred miles away. Those hills
make a damned good sanctuary for 'em, and they know it.'

'We found their hide-out without too much trouble,'
McCorg pointed out, 'And killed one of their number. But
there was no money there.'

'Then they must've hidden it someplace else.'

'That follows. And what makes you so certain they won't
pull up stakes and get out of the territory while they have
the chance?'

'Greed, Sheriff.' The banker smiled thinly. 'I know this
type of man. You've got to realize that even though they
picked up a large sum of money when they robbed that
train, when it's shared out among that bunch, they'll soon
be broke again. Money runs through their fingers like
water. A couple of weeks in Tucson and they'll be back for
more.'

'Somehow, I hope you're right,' McCorg said huskily. 'If
I figured they'd run for Mexico, I'd go out after them. But
you make it sound right.'

'What about this prisoner you brought in. Reckon he'll
talk?'

'Maybe. He's in a spot and he knows it. Maintains that
the bunch will ride into town and bust him out of jail
before we can bring him to trial, but deep down inside, I
don't think he believes that. If they was so all-fired
concerned about him, they'd have waited for him to move
with them instead of ridin' on without him like they did.'

Carew was brooding. 'I don't know,' he replied. 'I think
it more likely that they'd have a meeting place somewhere
up in those hills. And what do you figure they'll do once
they find out you know where their hide-out is and that
you killed the *hombre* they left to guard the place?'

'I'm hopin' it's taken them off their guard for a little
while, forced their hand. Maybe there'll be a showdown.'

Carew was dubious. He sat back in his chair and

regarded the other levelly for several moments in thoughtful silence. Then he said: 'Reckon it's only right you ought to know the feelin' in the town, Sheriff. You're the elected representative of the law around here and I wouldn't like you to—'

'Mr Carew,' McCorg said wearily. He sighed. 'I've been trailin' those killers for two days. I had no sleep whatever last night keepin' watch over my prisoner. I'm in no mood for guessin' games. If you've got somethln' to say, then spit it out instead of talkin' around things like this.'

For a moment, the other regarded him in silence with a hurt look on his face. Then he coughed, nodded. 'Very well. The point is this, Sheriff. Those three men who were kidnapped and then murdered were not citizens of Vendado, yet they were guests at the hotel here and there's a lot of bad feelin' against these killers. I'd just like to warn you that once the news gets around that you brought in one of 'em and you're holdin' him in the jail, folk may decide to take the law into their own hands and do somethin' they may regret later.'

'You're tryin' to say they may form a lynch mob, take him out and string him up without a proper trial?' McCorg raised his brows a little.

'That's it, Sheriff,' nodded the other. 'I don't agree with that course of action myself, please believe that. I'm for law and order. There is law here and there's a course of action laid down for events like this. This *hombre* is as guilty as hell of the charge of murder. You know that, I know it, and so does he. But his hangin' will have to wait until the circuit judge gets here in a few weeks' time.'

'Yet you're of the opinion that Fleck won't be alive by that time. That's it, isn't it?'

Carew, rubbed his chin slowly, stared down at the table under his other hand. 'Things sure look that way at the moment, Sheriff. Unless you take a hand right now before some folk start trouble. There are plenty of hotheads around who don't want to see justice done, rather they want excitement. They're the ones to watch right now.'

'Thanks for the warning,' said McCorg stiffly. Certainly this was the first time he had considered this threat to the law and order in Vendado. Maybe he ought to have realized that in a town such as this, one which had seen a great deal of violence in its short, stormy history, lynching of prisoners was something to be reckoned with.

'Just thought I'd better let you know,' murmured his companion. He remained silent as McCorg finished the stew and sipped the hot coffee at his elbow. Then he fished inside his waistcoat pocket and brought out a brace of cigars, handing one to the sheriff. They lit up in silence. Eyeing the other, McCorg found himself wondering what sort of man Carew was. Weak-willed, perhaps. A man who didn't wish to become embroiled in anything that smelled of danger, preferring to stand on the outer ring of spectators where there might be less danger. But there were a great many like him in these frontier towns and the rebuilding of the west might depend just as much on them as on the few true pioneers who would brave any danger for what they believed to be right.

'You know, Sheriff, I maybe should confess that when you were suggested for this post, I had my own personal misgivings. I did not think you were the right man for the job.'

McCorg glanced at the other in surprise. 'Why do you say that?' he asked.

The banker shrugged his shoulders. 'We'd had trouble with the Matagorda Kid and his men before you came. Stage hold-ups mostly. But I knew then that if they weren't stopped at the time, things would get worse until they might even take over the town. As banker here in town, I had to make a few inquiries, to satisfy myself as to your worth. I must confess I was a little surprised by some of the things I learned about you.'

'What sort of things?' McCorg asked sharply. He drew

deeply on the cigar, watched the red tip glow in the dimness of the restaurant.

In a quiet tone, the other went on: 'Your brother, for example. I know a lot about him. I—'

'I think you've said enough, Carew.' There was a note of veiled anger and menace in the other's tone. 'You got no right pokin' around into my affairs like that and—'

The other stiffened abruptly. Shortly, he said: 'For a man whose only brother ran off and joined up with a notorious band of outlaws, you're actin' mighty touchy, Sheriff.' He lowered his voice a little. 'I'm not the sort to hold it against any man what his kin are or do. But you can see my predicament when they suggested you for sheriff. Came to me then you might've got more sympathies with the outlaws than with the law-abidin' citizens.'

'Why you—' McCorg leaned across the table, grabbed the other by the front of the shirt and hauled him to his feet.

'All right, Sheriff; all right. I'm sorry I mentioned it. Nothing against you, you know.'

With a tremendous effort, McCorg released his hold on the other and forced down his wild anger. Where was an answer to what the other had said? It was true and he had no words to offer. Argue? Force the other back, take his anger out on this man? These were the easy ways to solve the problem. And they wouldn't really solve it. Wouldn't alter by one bit the fact that his brother had done just that. He wondered vaguely how it had come to this man's ears; how many other men in Vendado knew of it. It was a long silence, broken only by Carew's harsh breathing as he sucked air down into his heaving lungs in great, sobbing gasps.

'Hell, you well nigh killed me,' he managed to get out after a few moments. 'Reckon you'd better aim to control that all-fired temper of yours, Sheriff. You've got a job here, one we pay you to do and that doesn't include trying to kill men for tellin' the truth.'

McCorg stood by the table, watched the other turn on his heel, pick up his hat, clamp it down on his head, and stride pompously out of the restaurant. He felt dull and empty, weary to his bones, yet he knew there would be no real rest for him until this outlaw bunch had been rounded up and he had, in some small way, paid for what his brother had done all those years before.

Sitting down at the table, thrusting his legs out in front of him, sunk deep in thought, oblivious to everything that went on around him, he cast his mind back to that fateful day, almost eight years before. Until then, Jed had been a good boy, three years older than himself, honest and hard-working, riding herd on the ranch, mending the perimeter fences, attending to the general, everyday chores which went with life on a ranch.

Looking back on it, everything seemed sharp and clear-cut in his memory even though many later events were hazed by time and distance, had become shadowy and unreal.

The previous evening, Jed had ridden into town with some of the ranch hands, drinking at the Drover's Rest. There had been a bunch of men in the saloon, men who had ridden into town that afternoon from nobody-knew-where. Later, Clint had managed to piece together what had occurred from bits of information imparted by the ranch hands. Jed had got into conversation with these men, had been talking with them most of the evening and well into the night. Maybe the fact that Lucy Charleton had turned him down only three days earlier had had something to do with the decision he had reached. At least, Clint liked to think it had, for it made a little sense out of events which would otherwise have been utterly senseless and meaningless.

The next morning, when he and Jed had made their round of the ranch, checking on the herd and the fences, he had noticed there was something different about his brother, something he had not been able to put his finger on and apprise for sure, but which had worried him at the time. Jed had talked little, beyond mentioning that Lucy had obviously turned him down for someone else in town who had far more money and a better position than he would ever have if he continued to spend the rest of his life acting as nursemaid to a bunch of steers.

That evening, when they returned to the ranch house, Jed had gone into the bunkhouse, quietly collected together all of his gear, saddled up the best and fastest mount they owned and had ridden out without saying a word to anyone concerning his destination. When he failed to return the next morning, Clint had ridden into town to inquire about him and had learned that he had been seen riding out shortly after sundown with that same bunch of men to whom he had been talking the previous evening. Only then did he learn that these men were the notorious Benton gang, that Jed had evidently thrown in his lot with them, rather than go on working on the ranch.

That was the last they had heard of Jed for almost a year. Then the newspapers carried an account of a raid on the bank in Twin Falls. Two of the outlaws had been shot dead in the street outside the bank when they had tried to make their getaway, but the others had escaped with almost twenty thousand dollars, leaving behind two cashiers and a guard critically wounded. The description of one of the outlaws seen fleeing from the scene of the crime had fitted Jed exactly. The shock of this had been the cause of their mother's death.

Until that moment she had refused to believe that he was implicated in these robberies, but this news had been enough to make her take to her bed and she had died a few weeks later. He and his father had buried her on the low grassy knoll which overlooked the house, had laid her to rest in the earth she had loved so well. His father had lived for another two years and had then passed on, a broken man, his world lying in ruins about him.

'Don't let Carew bother you, Sheriff.' McCorg jerked

his head upright suddenly, saw that Chinese Charley had come quietly forward and was now standing beside the table, looking down at him concernedly. 'He likes to make people think he is important. Deep down, he is just a little man.'

'Thanks, Charley. I guess I was thinkin' too much of things that are in the past when I ought to be thinkin' about the present.'

'Sometimes,' said the other with a faint smile on his inscrutible features, 'the lessons that we learn from the past are useful in shaping our futures.'

'I'll try to remember that,' McCorg nodded, tossed a couple of coins on to the table and scraped back his chair. 'Reckon I'd better get back to the jail and see how my prisoner is gettin' on. Bring a tray across in an hour or so, Charley.'

'Sure thing, Sheriff.' The other nodded, pushed the coins into the pocket of his greasy shirt, and went back to his usual stance behind the counter.

As he entered the office, a slender figure, standing by the window, turned to face him. He closed the door softly behind him and pulled off his hat. 'Mary, what brings you here? I thought you'd still be workin' in the store.'

'I had to come, Clint.' She moved right up to him, placed her hands on his elbows and turned him to face her. 'There's talk going around that you have a prisoner in the cells, one of those men who killed Finney and the others. Is that true?'

'I guess so. I brought one man in a while ago. I've reason to believe that he was ridin' with those outlaws.'

'Gifford and some of the others are in the saloon now whipping up feeling against this man. There may be trouble. I wanted to warn you.'

Clint smiled thinly. 'I've already been warned, Mary,' he said quietly. He went over to the window and stared out into the street. 'Carew came to the restaurant to tell me there would be trouble, that there's a plan afoot to take Fleck out of jail and lynch him.'

'Believe me, if Gifford talks them over, they'll do it, Clint.'

He shook his head slowly. 'He's my prisoner, Mary. And if any lynch mob comes to the jail to take him out, then I'll be forced to fire on 'em. My duty is to protect this man until the circuit judge gets here and he receives a proper trial. I know he's guilty, but that makes no difference to what I have to do. I could have shot him down out there in the hills, but instead I brought him in for trial. Besides' – he added the last in a lower tone – 'I think I can get him to talk, tell us what the plans of the others are. My guess is that they still don't know we have him here.'

She was rigid for a long time, just watching his face. Then she leaned across to him and he felt the cool softness of her lips on his own. 'I knew you'd say that, Clint,' she murmured quietly. 'And I know that what you're doing is right, but it won't be easy. When they get their fill of liquor, these men will do anything. And once they've banded themselves together under a leader like Gifford, they're as bad as any outlaws. They want to take the law into their own hands and give out rough justice. The fact that everybody knows this man is guilty, won't help matters.'

'I'm afraid you're right.' He listened intently, could just make out the muted shouting from the saloon across the street. He could imagine what was happening in there. Gifford, the loud-mouthed ranch owner, buying booze for anyone who wanted it, talking a lot of high-faluting words about the law and justice, warning the others that unless they took the law into their own hands and strung up the prisoner in the jail, the chances were that he would be taken out by the rest of the gang and thereby escape his just deserts. In these frontier towns, the administration of the law was necessarily slow. There was only the one judge for a vast part of the territory and it took several months for him to make a complete circuit of the towns on his list. Often, this meant that a man would be kept locked in a cell for weeks, if not months, before being brought to trial and sentenced.

'Better get Costello, Gavin and Brick Williams, if you can find 'em, Mary. Would you do that for me. They're all men I can trust.'

'I'll go right away, Clint.'

'You know where Menderer is? I left him here when I stepped along the street for a bite to eat.'

'He's in the back with the prisoner.' She nodded towards the door on the far side of the office.

'Thanks. Now try to get those men as quickly as you can, Mary. Tell them what you told me. They'll know what the score is.'

She slipped out into the street. He heard her footsteps on the boardwalk outside the building, and a moment later, caught sight of her slender figure as she hurried over to the far side of the street. There was still no sign of trouble from the direction of the saloon, and McCorg had the feeling that it would be some time before that mob came to the jail. Gifford would take no chances on any of them backing down at the last moment. He himself, would remain in the background, taking no chance on getting any buckshot if it did come to shooting, but ready to urge on the others if they showed any signs of faltering. His lips curled derisively as he thought of the other. If there was any kind of man he despised it was the type who made loud deeds with his mouth but refused to back them up, preferring others to do it for him.

Menderer came in from the corridor. He said: 'You look all in, Clint. Why don't you take a few hours' sleep. I'll keep watch over Fleck.'

McCorg shook his head. 'There could be trouble – and soon,' he said. 'Real big trouble. Gifford is shootin' off his mouth in the saloon yonder, tryin' to get a mob together to lynch the prisoner.'

Menderer set his lips tight. 'So that's the way of it,' he said harshly. 'I didn't have it figured that they'd try it so soon. And why Gifford? What's his connection with this?'

'I only wish I knew. Maybe he figures that if he gets Fleck hung from the nearest cottonwood, he'll be a big man in the eyes of the townsfolk, the kind of man who really gets things done. Folk would listen to him then, and take less notice of their sheriff, who merely protected a killer.'

'What do you intend to do if they do come?' There was no fear, no apprehension in the other's tone, merely curiosity.

'Hold 'em off. At gunpoint if necessary. If they don't take a warnin', then some of 'em may get a load of buck-shot in their pants for their trouble.'

Menderer grinned. 'Two of us against maybe a couple of dozen?' He lifted his thick, bushy brows. 'Those aren't the best of odds, I reckon.'

'I've sent Mary out for three more. I figure the five of us should be enough for men like these, especially with loaded shotguns. Nobody in their right minds likes to face up to those guns.'

'And Gifford. What'll he be doin' while we're holdin' off the others?'

'You've got a point there. Knowing him, he could be sneakin' around the back, hopin' to get in a shot through the cell window.'

'You want me to keep a look-out back there if trouble starts?'

'Reckon you'd better,' McCorg said serenely. 'The four of us should be enough for the crowd in the street.'

Mary arrived with the three deputies five minutes later. Close on their heels, Doc Weaver hurried in. In answer to McCorg's inquiring glance, he said: 'I heard this prisoner of yours was wounded, Sheriff. Figured you might need me to take a look at him.' As he spoke, his arm brushed back the flap of his coat, revealing the heavy Colt thrust into his waist band.

'You figurin' on shootin' him, Doc?' Clint asked quietly, nodding towards the pistol.

The other hesitated, then went on a trifle shame-facedly: 'I heard a rumour goin' around that there might be an attempt to lynch this man. Not being a man of violence myself, I thought you might need help to prevent any breaking out.'

Clint grinned. 'Thanks, Doc. But you don't need to put yourself into any danger. I reckon we can take care of this bunch if they put in an appearance.'

'Well, I guess I can take a look at the prisoner, anyway?'

'Sure thing, Doc.' Costello led the way at a nod from McCorg.

Clint turned to the girl. 'If these men carry out their threat, this will be no place for you, Mary,' he said softly. 'You'd better get back to the store.'

'But I—'

'Please go, Mary. I'd feel a lot better in my mind if I knew you were safe. I doubt if we'll have any trouble. These men usually back down once they find themselves facing guns.'

'Very well.' She hesitated. 'But please take care, Clint. There's still a lawless element around town and they aren't all outlaws. They'll follow any man who plies them with enough drink and probably pays them to do his dirty work, while he stays in the background and takes all of the credit.'

'I'll watch myself.' He squeezed her arm affectionately, led her towards the door, closing it behind her. Then he turned towards the others. 'Better break out the shotguns, men,' he said. 'If they get really riled up on liquor, they may be the only weapons that'll stop 'em in their tracks. I don't want any bloodshed if I can help it. These men are, after all, citizens of the town. A little misguided in their loyalties perhaps, easily swayed, but not on the same level as the killers we're huntin'.'

Brick Williams nodded as he opened the lock on the shotguns, took them down from the wall rack and handed them out while Gavin broke open the packet of shells. 'There are times, when I think these lynch mobs are doin' a good job. They save the judge, jury and executioner work and the town a heap of money. Especially when the prisoner is known to be guilty without a shadow of doubt.'

'Maybe if things were different, I'd agree with you,' McCorg conceded, 'but that man in the cell means more to me than just a prisoner. He knows a lot that could be important to us and I mean to find out what it is, even if I have to pistol-whip it out of him.'

Williams grinned a little, took up his station at the window where he could watch the street. He held the shotgun between his hands, his sharp features creased with wrinkles as he screwed up his eyes against the sunlight that now slanted into the building.

'Somethin' happening yonder now,' he said ten minutes later. 'Looks like a big crowd headed this way.'

Clint joined him at the window. The batwing doors of the saloon had been thrown open and a score of men poured out into the street. Several still clutched whiskey bottles in their hands, some loosed off shots into the air. Shifting his gaze a little, he looked for Gifford, saw the other a moment later, coming out of the saloon with his usual sauntering gait. He remained standing on the boardwalk, looking down into the street, pulling on his gloves. There was a faint smirk on his face as he stared across in the direction of the sheriff's office.

'Let's hope that Menderer keeps a close watch back there,' he said through his teeth. 'My bet is that Gifford isn't expectin' this mob to get to Fleck. All he wants them to do is keep us occupied while he sneaks around to the back like the little rat he is.'

Even as he spoke, the ranch owner stepped down off the boardwalk and moved away from the crowd, edging along the street.

While most of the crowd milled aimlessly in the street outside the sheriff's office, two of the men, swarthy, black-bearded men, stamped up to the door and hammered loudly on it.

A harsh voice yelled: 'Bring out that killer, Sheriff. We've got our own brand of justice for him.'

'Watch the windows,' McCorg ordered. Gripping the shotgun tightly in his hands, he stepped to the door, threw it open, then closed it behind him as he faced the crowd.

'You got somethin' on your mind, Mister?' he asked levelly, staring at the nearest man. The barrel of the gun lowered a little until it was pointed directly at the other's chest.

'We're goin' to take that killer off your hands, Sheriff,' said the other tightly. He swallowed thickly, his close-set eyes narrowed a little. It was clear that he did not now relish the position of spokesman for the mob, not with McCorg's finger tight on the trigger, needing just a slight touch to blast him into eternity. The destructive power of a single barrel of shot was enough to kill several men, to shred their bodies to a mangled pulp that was scarcely recognizable as anything human. He now took a step backward, almost lost his balance as his spurs caught in one of the boards.

'You're goin' to disperse quietly, or I'll be forced to make sure that you do,' Clint said evenly. 'There are three more shotguns pointed at you from the windows at my back and each man has orders to shoot the minute I give the word.'

'Now be reasonable, Sheriff,' broke in one of the other men in the crowd. ' We don't want no trouble with you, but you know as well as any of us that this *hombre* you got in there is one of the men who killed those three strangers. You aim to give him board and lodgin' at our expense just so's the circuit judge can make everythin' legal.'

'That's exactly what I aim to do.'

'You can't kill all of us, Sheriff,' snarled the black-bearded man thinly. 'And I figure it ain't worth losin' your life just to protect a killer.'

'You're forgotten' somethin', mister,' Clint said quietly.

The other regarded him closely for a moment. 'What's that?' he asked finally.

'That this gun is trained on your chest right now. I'm givin' this lynch mob exactly ten seconds to start driftin' away and then you get the first barrel. If there are any men left after we've finished, to go in there and take that prisoner out, you won't be around to see it.'

'Now just a minute, Sheriff. Like I said, we've got nothin' against you. All we want is that *hombre* in there. You just turn your back for a few minutes, take a walk to the restaurant. It'll all be over by the time you get back.'

'Ten seconds,' said Clint ominously. There was a sharp click as he pulled back the hammer. There was tension in the breeze that flowed along the street of Vendado. Among the crowd, McCorg saw that there were faces tight with challenge, eyes fixed on the man who faced him, waiting for a sudden move from the other that could start guns roaring. Moving his head slowly, Clint let his sharp gaze wander over the faces of the others in the dusty street. The slanted sunlight etched their features with shadow, highlighted the planes of their faces.

But, when the interruption came, it came not from the street, but from the narrow alley that ran alongside the jail. The sudden, sharp crack of a pistol, shattering the stillness into a thousand screaming fragments. There came a harsh cry close on the heels of the single shot. Clint turned his head sharply, knew that for the moment there was nothing to fear from the men facing him. There was a moment of silence. Then the slow, shuffling sound of footsteps in the dry dust.

As one man, the crowd turned, their mission there temporarily forgotten by this new turn of events. There was a movement at the corner of the building. First a shadow and then the swaying body of the man who clawed at the wall for support, who staggered and then fell sideways into the street, arms coming to rest on the edge of the boardwalk at the corner.

For a moment, the men stared at the fallen figure. Then somebody yelled loudly: 'It's Gifford. He's been shot.'

Lowering the shotgun, Clint walked slowly along the boardwalk until he stood above the inert body. The other's face was turned sideways and he could make out the thin lips, drawn back over the teeth in a snarling grimace of agony.

'Somebody get Doc Weaver,' called another man, on his knees beside the rancher. 'He's still breathin' but hurt bad.'

'The Doc's inside the jail,' Clint told them. 'Takin' a look at the prisoner.'

'One of you men go get him,' said Gilman, short and stocky foreman of the Gifford spread. He rubbed his glistening forehead with the back of his hand, then glanced up at McCorg, face serious now, no longer quite so flushed with the whiskey. 'This is a bad business, Sheriff. We didn't figure on any shootin' when we came over here.'

'Guess you should remember that whenever there's a lynch mob roamin' the streets of a town, there'll always be shootin'. They go together.'

'But who'd want to shoot Gifford?' asked the other, his tone perplexed.

'I reckon it was Menderer, my deputy,' said Clint, eyeing the other levelly. 'Actin' on my orders,' he went on quickly as he saw the hardening of the other's face. 'I guessed that Gifford would take the opportunity of waitin' until we were all arguing out here to sneak around the back and try to get off a lucky shot into the cell. All that bothered him was makin' sure this *hombre* died. It didn't matter if it was by the rope or a bullet. So I had Menderer stationed inside the cell with orders to shoot if anybody tried anythin' like that. And the same goes for anybody else who tries to take my prisoner out of jail before the judge gets here.'

'You figurin' on watchin' over him every hour of the day and night, Sheriff? Somehow, I don't reckon you can.'

Clint smiled thinly. 'Don't have to,' he said evenly. 'I've only to wire to Tucson that there's trouble here and there'll be so many troopers and federal men swarming in Vendado, you'll find yourself off the streets. This robbery has brought things to a head. Now you'd better disperse quietly, or I'll put half of you in jail for disturbin' the peace.'

The men hesitated, shuffling their feet. When Doc Weaver came out of the building and walked slowly along the boardwalk to where Gifford lay, they broke into little knots of men, moving uneasily, eyeing the shotgun under McCorg's arm and then the sprawled body in the dust. The shooting of the rancher seemed to have stunned and subdued them; they had lost all of their desire for a show-down now. Stepping forward, Clint said: 'How is he, Doc?'

'Pretty bad, but I reckon he'll live,' muttered the other. 'Get a door some of you and carry him into the saloon yonder where I can take a better look at him. And be careful how you handle him, that bullet is mighty close to the lung and any sudden jolt could mean the end for him.'

A door was brought, Gifford laid on to it, and he was carried across into the saloon. McCorg waited until the crowd had dispersed, then stepped inside the office. Menderer came in from the back. He glanced directly at McCorg.

'I had to shoot him, Clint,' he said tightly. 'He tried to draw a bead on Fleck through the cell window. I shouted to warn him but he took no notice.'

'Think nothin' more of it,' Clint told him. 'He asked for everythin' he got. The Doc is lookin' at him now. He reckons he'll live, but it'll be some time before he steps up into the saddle again.'

'What about the rest of 'em?' queried Brick Williams.

He still stood at the window, gripping the shotgun tightly in his fists, staring through the dusty pane of glass towards the saloon.

'I doubt if we'll have any further trouble from them for the time being,' Clint said, placing the shotgun against the wall. 'They only came lookin' for trouble because Gifford plied them with drink and did a lot of fancy talkin'. Now that he's out of the way for some time, they'll forget all about this little incident.'

'And Fleck?'

'I mean to have a little pow-wow with him right now.' Clint moved across the room, walked quickly along the corridor to the cell that housed the outlaw. He stared in through the bars for a moment, eyeing the other up and down before speaking.

It was Fleck who spoke first. His tone was even as he said disinterestedly. 'Sounded like a little trouble out in the street, Sheriff. You know you should control these towns-folk better'n that.'

'Maybe I should have let them come in and take you.'

Fleck shook his head slowly, confidently. 'You wouldn't have done that, Sheriff. I'm a pretty good judge of character and I know your type. If you'd wanted me dead, you'd have used your gun to better effect back there in the hills. You'll see to it that I'm still around to stand my trial.'

'Sure,' said Clint thoughtfully, keeping his eyes on the other's face. 'You'll still be here, but I won't guarantee your physical condition.'

Fleck swung his legs to the floor, sat up on the edge of the bunk. He had temporarily lost his sudden confidence. 'What is that supposed to mean, lawman?' he said harshly.

'Just that I believe you know where your companions are headed, where you had arranged to meet them to share out the proceeds from that train robbery. I want to know where the meeting place is and who the other men in the gang are.'

The other grinned thinly. 'And you think I'm goin' to

tell you.' He shook his head, lay down again on the bunk. 'You're ridin' the wrong trail there, Sheriff. I'm sayin' nothing.'

'There are ways of makin' a stubborn man talk,' Clint said softly, very softly.

'You're bluffin',' The other clasped his hands behind his neck and stared up complacently at the ceiling.

Clint's glance went to the men in the corridor and his face still bore part of a smile. 'Any of you men know where Chickasaw Pete is right now?'

'Most likely around one of the stores,' said Gavin. 'That's where he usually hangs out durin' the afternoon.'

'Fetch him.'

Gavin hurried off. Out of the corner of his eye, Clint noticed Fleck watching him with an expression of growing concern on his face. He still lay stretched out on the bunk, but he no longer appeared sure of himself. 'Time's gettin' on, Fleck,' said Clint quietly. 'I don't have any to waste. You've never met Chickasaw Pete before, I reckon. He still remembers most of the habits of his people as you'll soon discover if you won't talk.'

'You're just tryin' to scare me.' Fleck's voice was shaking a little. He got to his feet, holding on to the side of the bunk to stand upright, rubbing the bandage around his injured leg.

Clint shrugged unconcernedly. He already knew the kind of man he was dealing with, knew that even the thought of torture at the hands of a Chickasaw would be enough to break the other. Williams said suddenly. 'Here comes Chickasaw Pete now.'

Fleck's eyes switched towards the far end of the corridor, wide and bulging. The Indian came forward slowly, gaze moving from one man to another until it fastened on Clint.

'What is this, Sheriff?' he asked haltingly. 'I done nothing.'

'We need your help, Pete,' Clint said, taking his arm

and leading him forward. 'We think this man has information which is important to us. We want you to make him talk. I don't care how you do it – just do it!'

SIX
Gunhawk

Through the grilled door of the cell, Clint McCorg stared in at the prisoner. Fleck was lying on the bunk with the rough blanket drawn up over his body so that only his arms and head were visible. Smiling a little to himself, he moved back into the outer office. Menderer and Brick Williams were seated at the small table playing cards with a grubby deck. They glanced up as he entered the room.

'You reckon he was tellin' the truth about those other *hombres*, Clint,' Williams flicked the grey length of ash from the end of his cigarette.

Clint nodded. 'Chickasaw Pete didn't have to do much to him before he started shootin' off his mouth. He was scared spitless, believe me. That trail he spoke about, the old Turral Mine. Either of you know it?'

'Heard of it,' said Menderer quietly. He took a card from the pack in front of him, sat staring at it for a long moment without any expression on his face. 'It's the kind of place they'd go if they'd decided to leave their other hide-out. From what I've heard, the place would be damned nearly impregnable. They used burros along some of those trails when the mine was open and yieldin' gold. But that was more'n fifteen years ago. Nobody's been near the place since then that I know of.'

Williams gave a quick nod of confirmation. 'Reckon

that's the truth, Clint. It's one hell of a place, way up in the hills. Only man who might know about it is Clem Roderick. He knows these hills like the back of his hand.'

Clint stood silent, assimilating that. It was difficult to say how Roderick might react if he asked him to lead them up to the old Turral Mine, especially if the other guessed their reasons for going there.

'You know where Clem might be at this moment?'

Williams glanced at the darkening sky outside. 'I'd say he'll be in Chinese Charley's, gettin' a bite to eat before goin' across to the saloon to be parted from what little dust he's got left in that saddle-bag of his.' He grinned. 'Get him when he's at rock bottom, Clint, and he'll do anythin' for money or whiskey.'

Nodding, Clint went out into the street. Already, dusk was beginning to settle over Vendado. The sun vanished behind the distant hills with a flash of red and crimson that was like a vast upsurging fire over the far rim of the world, throwing its streamers out into the heavens while the encroaching darkness of night came sweeping in out of the east and the first stars were just becoming visible near the zenith.

There was an occasional light burning out of a square window along the length of the street but nothing else showed along the boardwalks except for the odd loafer, getting the last of the warmth out of the evening air before going inside. He waked one of the sleeping men in a high backed rocker, in front of one of the stores, recognized Mary Kenner's father. The other gave him a quick nod, rose to his feet as he came level with him.

'Evenin', Sheriff,' he greeted. 'Heard there was a little ruckus at the jail a while ago. No real trouble, I hope.'

Clint gave a shake of his head. 'Nothin' we couldn't handle,' he said easily. 'Some hotheads tried to take my prisoner out and lynch him. Gifford got himself shot in the chest in the attempt.'

'Gifford,' murmured the other musingly. 'Bad man to tangle with, Sheriff.'

'Afraid I've got more on my mind to worry me than Gifford.'

A glinting expression appeared on the other's face. 'The Matagorda Kid?'

'Yes,' said Clint. 'We know he's up there in the hills near the old Turral mine.'

'You aim to ride up there after him?' There was surprise in Kenner's tone. 'Evidently you don't know that part of the hills.'

'I'm hopin' that Clem Roderick will know, and that he'll agree to lead us there.'

The other twisted his lips for a moment in deep thought, then went on softly: 'They taken Gifford out of town, back to his ranch, Sheriff?'

For a moment, the question took the other off balance, then he caught himself abruptly. 'I wouldn't know,' he said, beginning to move on. 'Why do you ask?'

'Just a feelin' I got. It's as quiet as a graveyard in town tonight. Not a goddamned soul in sight.'

He found Roderick without effort, seated at one of the tables in the small restaurant, eating his evening meal. The old prospector glanced up curiously as the other seated himself in the chair opposite. He watched the other in silence for a moment, then motioned to Chinese Charlie to bring a bottle and a couple of glasses. After the other had set them down on the table and gone, he poured a couple of drinks, looked directly at Roderick over the rim of his glass and said: 'How'd you like to earn yourself a few dollars, Clem?'

'Doin' what?' inquired the other, staring down at the liquor in front of him.

'Leadin' me and a posse up into the hills.'

Roderick's eyes narrowed a little as he digested that. 'Where would you be wantin' to go, Sheriff? Seems to me you've got somethin' on your mind.'

'You know the old Turral mine?' Clint asked directly,

watching the other's face for any sign of reaction to the question.

'Sure, I know it,' nodded Roderick. He looked puzzled, perplexed. 'What's your interest in that place?'

'I want to get there and as quickly as possible. Leavin' tonight.' The old prospector looked at him with some care. 'You sure you know what you're askin', Sheriff? That ain't no place to go foolin' around with, even in daylight. After dark, only a fool would try that trail.' He gulped down the whiskey, rubbed his beard with the back of his hand. 'I suppose you got some real good reason for wantin' to go there?'

'Yes,' said Clint tightly.

'Such as hopin' to find that outlaw gang holed up in the mine workings?' It was more of a statement than a question. There was a shrewd gleam in the other's eyes.

'All right. So that's the reason. What do you say? Will you lead us?'

'Hell,' breathed the other. He rolled a cigarette, lighted it and drew in a breath of smoke. Then he pointed at Clint. 'You're buckin' your luck, Sheriff. And on two counts. That mining trail goes up through a canyon with damned steep sides, then skirts around the side of the hill with a sheer three hundred foot drop on one side. You get halfway along there, find a slide blockin' the trail and how are you goin' to get back? Last time I went along it, I came across this break, nearly ten feet across. It's nothin' to fool around with in daylight. Then you got these *hombres* to think about. They'll know you've brung in one of their number and that in all probability he's talked. Every inch of that trail will be watched. If they are there, it'd take an army to prise 'em out.'

'We're not likely to get that sort of help,' Clint retorted. 'It struck me though that if this trail is as bad as you say, things could work both ways.'

Roderick wrinkled his brows in deep thought. 'I don't get your meanin', Sheriff,' he muttered finally.

Clint sighed. 'If it's goin' to be difficult for us to get up there without bein' seen, it'll be just as difficult for them to get down. We'll have 'em bottled up before dawn if you agree.'

'Well . . .' The other was still dubious. 'All right, I'll do it. I only hope I live long enough to drink some of that money.' He wanted to refuse this, would have refused it, but for the fact that the other would have looked on him as a coward.

'I'll meet you outside the sheriff's office in half an hour.' Clint got to his feet.

Outside, in the street, he was on the point of returning to the office, when he bumped into Mary Kenner. As he moved close, she said almost breathlessly, 'Brick Williams says that you're thinking of going up into the hills tonight after the rest of that gang. Don't do it, Clint. They could ambush you and kill every man in the posse before you knew they were there. There will be too many for you to fight and they'll have every advantage on their side.'

'That's a risk we have to take,' he said softly. 'You'll find that the world can be a cruel and brutal thing and very often one has to be equally brutal in order to shape it into what you want. If there is to be any decency and honesty at all, people have to take risks, make sacrifices, and some people have to give their lives. There's a curse on a rich, new country like this. A curse that's been put on it by ourselves. Maybe there was something big and wonderful and clean about it all once, and maybe there will be again, but right at this moment in our history, everything is rotten and dirty, has to be scoured and scoured.'

She looked at him in silence for a long moment. 'I never thought you were a man who thought of things so deeply as this.'

'When you ride the long trails along with only your own thoughts and ideas to keep you company, then you get to thinking of such things,' he said. 'The big trouble is that you can never go back and ride over a part of the trail for a second time, maybe change some things in the light of what you now know.'

'Where do you want to go back to, Clint?' she murmured softly, her eyes searching his face in the shadows as if expecting, and hoping, to find an answer to her question there.

'A great many places and times.' He was silent for a long moment, and there were the shadows of trouble around his eyes, drooping the corners of his mouth. He thought again of Jed, was surprised that there was none of the angry bitterness or remorse which he had experienced over the past years whenever he had thought of him.

'Are you sorry for having taken on the job of sheriff in Vendado?'

He hesitated for a moment, then shook his head. 'Someone has to do the job if there is to be law and order. I went into it with my eyes open, knowing most of what was expected of me.'

'It might be easier and safer if you were to ask for help from Tucson. The army could send troopers to go up into the hills with you.' She spoke quietly, thinking out of his sudden silence, knowing that she was making her point. 'It would only take two or three days and those outlaws would still be there at the end of that time.'

Clint shook his head. 'It would take two or three weeks, Mary,' he said earnestly, 'before all of the necessary documents had gone through the prescribed army channels. I know how the Army acts and thinks. And whatever happens, we can't afford to wait that length of time.'

'So you have to risk your life.' Her words fell dully into the stillness that hung like a velvet blanket over the street. She studied him briefly, then turned slowly away. 'I see that you have made up your mind about this and that nothing I can do or say is going to make you change it.'

'I'm sorry, Mary.' He knew that he was not making his case plain to her, that she was waiting for him to say he would hold off until more men arrived from Tucson; and equally, he knew that he could not wait, that if he failed now, he would never feel clean, would never want to wear the sheriff's badge again, could never walk through these streets with his head held high.

When she did not answer, he went on: 'Better go home now, Mary. I'll come back, I promise you.' He let go her arm, spun away and walked swiftly along the boardwalk to the jail.

A small group of riders sat their mounts in front of the building. He let his gaze roam over them, then motioned them down. 'Step inside, boys,' he called; 'there are a few things I want to talk over before we ride out.'

Turning up the lamp on the desk in the office, he got the bunch of keys down from their hook, went across to the strap-steel cages on the walls which housed the Winchesters and handed them out one by one. For a time, his unwavering gaze was riveted on the men in the office. They were earnest and hard men who knew the danger which faced them if they rode out with him on this mission; and who also knew the greater danger that faced the town, if not the entire territory, if they refused to go. He felt he could rely on them, knew they would carry out his orders. How many of them would be alive in twenty-four hours, he could not guess.

'Roderick goin' to help?' asked Brick Williams.

'Says he'll meet us here in a little while,' Clint answered. 'I reckon he will. He's sure a queer cuss, but if he gives his word, he'll keep to it.'

'Brick was sayin' that they may be holed up in the old Turral mine,' said one of the men, lounging against the wall beside the door. 'That's no place to go riding in the dark. Besides, they reckon it's been abandoned for more'n fifteen years, that even the trail up to it has been forgotten, lost. How come that this fellow Roderick knows where it is?'

Clint shrugged. 'He's roamed those hills from one end to the other for as long as anybody in this town can remember,' he replied. 'I reckon if anyone knows the trail, he does.'

'He's an old man,' went on the other stubbornly, not once taking his gaze from Clint. 'And at his age, men are inclined to be a mite forgetful. They start to imagine things, get their facts mixed up with their dreams, until they don't recall anythin' straight any more. How do we know the same thing won't happen again with him? Maybe, at one time, he did know that trail. But it could've been a long while ago and by now, he could've forgotten it. He could lose us in those goddamned hills and none of us would be any the wiser until it was too goshdarned late to do anythin' about it.'

'He's our only chance,' growled a bearded, older man standing near the desk. 'I'm against ridin' into any situation with my eyes shut, but if the sheriff here reckons there's a good chance then I'll ride with him.'

There was a faint murmur of assent from the rest of the men and as Clint looked towards the man near the door, the other shrugged his shoulders nonchalantly and said: 'That's all right by me, I guess. When do we ride?'

'As soon as Roderick turns up. Check that you have plenty of ammunition and food. There's plenty of water up there, and game too if we have to hang around for a time.'

'You reckonin' on being in the hills for some time then?' asked Gavin.

'Could be. I'm hopin' that if we can't attack them in the old mine workings, then we can hole 'em up there long enough to force 'em to come out.'

'That's goin' to be a mighty tall order.'

'I know.' He made to speak again, but at that moment, there was the sound of a rider reining up in front of the office. 'Time for us to go, I guess.'

They rode out of town in a tight bunch, headed north towards the long, low sweep of the foothills that stood out on the distant horizon, looming dark and strangely ominous against the night sky. The stars were glittering pinpoints of light against the deep velvet blackness. There would be a moon, thought Clint, as he rode beside Roderick, but it would not rise until early in the morning, and by that time, he hoped to be well inside the hills. Glancing at Roderick out of the corner of his eye, he saw the other's lips stretch thin, the ragged beard ruffling in the wind against his jacket. He had pulled up the high collar against the chill of the night wind, was bending forward in the saddle, hands tight on the reins, peering off into the clinging blackness that lay all around them, stretching away to the limitless horizons.

Two miles out of town, they hit a smooth, flat stretch of country and set their mounts into a steady canter. Mountain cold blew against them now and the ponderous weight of the hills threw itself against them. They approached the rising rimrocks of the lower range from the south-west and pushed swiftly upward without slowing their progress. Hurrying along the lip of a long, curving ridge, they moved directly up into jack-pine and manzanita, spurring their mounts now as they tended to flag. There was no trail to follow at this point, yet the prospector showed no concern at this. He stared straight ahead of him, scarcely conscious of the men who rode with him.

At last, however, the ground began to rise steeply. This was country of which Clint McCorg had no knowledge and he felt a momentary stab of surprise at the way in which the ground lifted, forming a narrow humped ridge and on either side of it, the ground dropped precipitously away and he had the impression that they were riding along a razor's edge where the slightest misstep could mean a neck-breaking fall into the tumbled rocks on either side.

'This the only way up into the hills from this direction?' Clint asked.

Roderick turned his head slightly. 'If you want to get there in the shortest possible time it is,' he replied.

'Besides, they won't be expectin' anybody to come this way. Only a fool would ride here in the darkness.'

'I can well believe that,' answered Clint fervently. He glanced down the slope that fell away sharply to his right. Rugged boulders had at some earlier time slid down the slope here, gouging a deep scar in the side of the ridge.

Now that they had embarked on this trail, there was no turning back. They had no choice but to go on. Scarcely able to see more than a few yards in front of him, he rode with his hips rammed into the cantle, legs thrust out straight and rigid in the stirrups. He did not lift his eyes, nor raise his head more than an inch or so during the whole time they were on the back of the ridge, fighting to maintain his balance in the saddle and make it easier on the horse as it fought its way over some of the roughest country he had ever known. Huge boulders occasionally blocked their path and they were forced to halt and move gingerly past them, the horses' hoofs slipping and grating on the treacherous ground. Not until they had moved down off the saddlebacked ridge and were on more level ground was he able to deepen and slow the sweep of air into his lungs. He grew aware that his heart was beating strongly and rapidly in his chest, hammering against his ribs as the horse began gradually to straighten up beneath the saddle. Twisting to look back, he saw that the rest of the posse, strung out now in single file, were still there, struggling a little to keep their balance as they rode down towards the broad valley which lay between them and the foothills, now looming close to the horizon.

Two miles further on and Roderick lifted his right arm. Clint edged up to him. 'There's the peak,' said the prospector, pointing. 'The big one that stands out above all of the others. The old Turral mine nestled just below the crests, about three hundred feet from the top.'

Clint eyed the sharply-pointed spire of rock that stood out, even at a distance of perhaps fifteen miles. 'It must be close on two thousand feet up,' he said harshly.

'That's right,' Clem nodded. 'Still think you can get up there in darkness?'

'I hadn't expected anythin' quite like this,' Clint conceded, 'but we can have a damned good try. The horses are fresh and sure-footed.' He meant to add that the Matagorda Kid and his men had also evidently done it, but kept the thought to himself. They would undoubtedly have done it in broad daylight, when the going would be easier.

They didn't use the spurs again, but allowed the horses to have their head. The hard pull over the ridge had taken a lot out of the mounts. Their shoulder muscles and flanks glistened with sweat, quivering from the exertion. Further on, they ran into a new menace. Thick, sticky shrub that caught at the horses' feet, making the going both painful and difficult for them. There was no way around it and they were forced to move more slowly than Clint would have liked, as they picked their way through it. All around them, the cool stillness pressed down on them from all sides, like an almost physical pressure. Far off, over the rim of the hills, the sky was becoming overcast, the bright stars blotted out by encroaching cloud.

'There's a storm brewin',' observed Menderer tightly. 'No moon tonight.'

'Maybe that's all for the best.' Thinking on this, Clint felt his spirits rise a little. He did not underestimate the difficulties they still had to face, but if they could get a little luck on their side, their chances of success would be considerably improved. A look-out in the pouring rain was not inclined to be as sharp-eyed and attentive as one who watched in dry conditions. Riding a loose rein once they came out of the low thicket, he urged his mount ahead. In spite of the long, dragging minutes, the distant hills seemed to be as far off as ever. He felt in a hurry now, restlessness rode with him. There was still the possibility to be faced that in spite of Chickasaw Pete's persuasion, Fleck had not told the truth when he had given them this information. Or that he had told the truth as he knew it, but that once it had been discovered he was missing, possibly a prisoner, the gang had decided to make a break for it and flee across the border with what money and valuables they had.

The thought increased the feeling of restless urgency which had been growing in him with every mile, but he knew better than to push the horses any harder across this type of terrain and by degrees the country grew rougher, more rocky and treacherous and the trees which had sprung up on their right, became more stunted, often twisted and warped into fantastically weird shapes. The rocks, too, lifted higher, fluted columns of red sandstone rising sheer from the valley floor, the forerunners of the hills proper. They held to the winding trail for as long as possible, then dropped into one of the long, narrow ravines, crossed it, climbed the other side and came out on to the next ridge.

No sooner had they entered the foothills than the storm broke. The wind which had blown up during the past few minutes, suddenly struck down at them with a violent fury and heavy raindrops fell around them, pattering off the rocks, striking their faces and the crowns of their hats; only a few of them at first and then it was as if a curtain of rain came rolling down the steep side of the hill to engulf them. The wind increased in its roaring, keening fury, whipping at their clothing, forcing them to crouch as low as possible in the saddle, leaning into it as it tore and slashed them, filled not only with the raindrops, but with dust and stones that brought blood whenever they struck a man on hands or face. The horses did not like it, shied away from the sheer rock walls as the wind, striking them, glanced off at an angle, swung them roughly, forcibly, towards the edge of the trail.

The ground grew rougher and, in the chill, rain-filled darkness, always more uninviting. Soft ground, churned into mud within seconds under their horses' feet. This was a place of weirdly silhouetted buttes, long stretches of rocky trails, then soft, shifting sand, made even more treacherous by the rain, gorges that slanted steeply and without warning in front of them, down which they were forced to put their mounts, leaning high in the saddle to prevent their horses from sliding down to the bottom in a tangle of flesh and broken bones.

Still it rained. The water slid under the folds of Clint's jacket, down his neck, squeezed into the tops of his boots, brought discomfort to their bodies and curses to their lips. If there was a moon that night, its radiance was lost completely behind the boiling beserk clouds that roamed the length and breadth of the heavens. Off in the distance, there was a sudden splash of harsh light as lightning flared across the sky, the glare reflected from the rising peaks that marched all around them out to the horizon. The savage rumble of thunder came a few moments later.

Roderick motioned Clint forward, reining up his mount a little. He leaned sideways in the saddle, shouted the words so as to be heard above the furious racket of the storm. 'River's not far ahead,' he yelled. 'May be up because of the rain. Snow's been meltin' too.'

'How far ahead?'

'Half a mile, maybe.' The other rubbed the rain off his face where it streamed from the curved brim of his hat and ran on to his cheeks. 'Long time since I rode this trail, but it's one you ain't likely to forget once you've ridden it.'

'You're sure we're on the right trail?' Clint asked.

The other looked indignant. 'Course I'm sure,' he said, half angrily. 'I know these hills better than most folk knows the streets of Vendado.'

Ten minutes later, they came in sight of the river. Like the other had said, it was up. Rain and melting winter snow at the crests had done their work only too well. White water that was churned to foam in the rocky narrows, bubbling and churning as the strong current carried it down the hillside. The banks had been eroded during long ages of flood and as yet, there was little overflow over the banks.

For a moment, he felt a premonition of disaster if they dared to put their mounts into the river, then he brushed the thought away angrily. The men sat their horses along the bank and considered the situation. They looked on with interest as Clint suddenly rode his horse into the narrows close to the bank, then urged it further out into the main current that came surging down the rocky bed. Water foamed against the animal's chest, thrusting at it with an almost irresistible force. Near the middle, the bed fell away abruptly and Clint held the reins high as the horse began to swing diagonally across the high-running river towards the far bank. Somehow, he made it, sat for a moment, then signalled the others to come on. One by one, they entered the water, made the slow, dangerous crossing. Finally they were all on the bank, water streaming from them, dripping from their boots.

More thunder and lightning in the raging heavens but now they were in the tall timber and the thickly interwoven branches above their heads formed a thick umbrella which kept most of the rain off them, although the air under the trees was bitterly cold and strong. They sat shivering in their saddles as they walked their mounts forward, eyes alert for trouble now.

'The rain won't last much longer,' Gavin murmured. 'The wind has changed and we'll only get the rim of it now.'

The trees began to thin as they rode higher and when they finally came out of them, Clint saw that the other was right. Already, low down in the north-west, there was a wide clear stretch of sky, with the stars beginning to shine more brightly than before in it, as though the passing of the storm had somehow washed them clean. The rain slackened appreciably and then ceased altogether as the last of the clouds drifted swiftly towards the south, leaving only a cold wind blowing against them, cutting through their soaked clothing like a knife, numbing and chill.

It was not easy, going across the mountain slopes. Up the arching shoulder of one rugged outcropping of rock, then down into a gulch or ravine that opened up without warning in a patch of black shadow, then up again, with the narrow, dimly-seen trail twisting towards the high, sky-reaching peak all of the time.

Higher and higher, they rose with the sharply-curved switchback courses until a little after one o'clock, the moon rose in the east and shed its cold, clear radiance over the terrain around them.

'We'll be comin' close to that break in the trail any minute now,' Roderick said thinly. 'Better keep your eyes open for it. Can be real mean if you come on it unawares.'

They came upon it fifteen minutes later. It showed up faintly as a darker shadow across the narrow trail. Clint eased his mount forward ahead of the others until it stopped short and refused to go any further, but began to move around with slow, delicate mincing steps, winding about on the narrow ledge until it had almost turned around completely. Slipping from the saddle, he went forward the rest of the way on foot, bent as he came to the break. There was a broad slide of earth and rock immediately in front of it, jutting out across the trail almost from one side to the other and it was this, rather than the break itself which had caused the moonthrown shadow giving them warning of its presence.

Menderer came inching forward, his back and shoulders pressed tightly against the rock face as he stared down at the wide gap in the trail. 'Hell,' he said harshly. 'It must be the best part of five feet across. We'll have to clear the slide first before we can get the horses to take it.'

Clint straightened up, stood for a moment looking down at his feet. The flooding moonlight lit the trail itself at this point, but the canyon that lay just beyond the edge was in deep midnight shadow and no details whatever could be made out in the yawning blackness.

'What troubles me is, if it's such an old break that Roderick knows of it, how did the Matagorda Kid and the rest of his men get across it? Even in daylight, it would be very near impossible.'

'It would be a helluva sight easier than it is now,' the other retorted. 'You still goin' to try it before dawn?'

Without answering, Clint lifted his head and stared up in the direction of the looming peak that pressed down upon them with its ponderous, tremendous weight. Even looking at it, etched against the moonlit heavens, gave him a queer feeling. He shivered as cold gusts of air struck him. 'We'll make it,' he said at length. 'Stay here until I take a closer look at it.' Shuffling his feet cautiously, he edged towards the end of the slide, got down on his hands and knees and reached out with his arm into the dark shadow. Carefully, he scraped away the soft earth and boulders that barred any progress, until there was a clear path where he could just slide forward. Gingerly, he inched his way along the trail, squeezing past the slide. Once, his foot slipped off the edge and he clung to the rocks for dear life, his breath whooshing out of his lungs, his heart thudding violently against his ribs. He kicked violently at the rock face with the toe of his boot until he had made himself a small purchase and then levered himself up on to the trail once more. For a long moment, he sat quite still with his back pressed hard against the wall of earth and rock, breathing the cold air down into his lungs in great heaving gulps. For a moment, there was a feeling of deathly defeat in him.

Maybe the Matagorda Kid and the others had not come this way, always assuming they were at the Turral mine. Roderick was an old man. He could not be expected to know of every criss-crossing trail in these hills, no matter how much of his life he had spent up here. He recalled that they had seen no sign of horses along the trail since they had started up towards the towering summit. Lifting himself gently, he anchored himself firmly with his legs, crawled forward until he was past the slide. The break in the trail faced him now and he saw one thing that had a heartening effect on him. It was not, as he had anticipated, a complete break. There had obviously been a geological fault here and part of the outjutting trail had slid down into the chasm, leaving a ragged edge but even at its narrowest, there was still about two and a half feet of rock jutting from the side of the cliff.

He would have liked to have lit a match to take a better look, but it would have been too big a risk. Even the brief flare of a match could be seen for a great distance in the darkness. It was narrow, dangerous, but considering the girth of a horse, he thought there was the chance of moving along the break, leading the horses. So long as none of the brutes panicked in the darkness, they would be all right. Stepping out slowly, he tested the ledge for footing. It seemed firm enough, lasted for about ten feet, until the trail widened again. Not too big a break but enough to be troublesome during daylight, a hundred times worse at night.

'How does it look?' asked Menderer, when he went back to join the others.

'Not good,' he admitted. 'But I reckon we can make it. The break itself starts just beyond the slide. It's about ten feet in length and the trail is only a little more than a couple of feet wide. I figure we'd best move across leadin' the horses. A tight rein until they round the slide and on the break and then a loose rein so they can see the ground.' He paused, went on: 'I'll go first. Then you. The rest come over at intervals. Whatever happens, don't let the horses panic. That'll be fatal.'

He reached for the reins of his mount, pulled gently on them, coaxing the horse along the trail. At the slide, he hesitated, speaking softly and gently to the animal, to allay any panic. Backing around the slide, he kept the reins short and tight in his hands until his mount was around the bulging outcropping of earth and stone, facing the break. Here, it stopped, put down its head, sniffed at the ground beneath its forefeet and emitted a loud, sighing blast of air through its nostrils.

'Steady, boy,' Clint said soothingly. 'You're nearly there. Just a little way to go and you're across.'

He inched his way backward, feeling carefully with his heels before putting any weight on his feet. A stone underfoot slipped away from him, rattled to the edge and then went over. He heard it bouncing down the slope, striking the rocks on the way down. It seemed to keep on falling for a long time before it hit the bottom and there were only the faint, hard echoes chasing themselves across the chasm. More than two hundred feet, he thought with a little shiver. A man and his horse went over there and there would be very little left of them once they hit the bottom.

Pulling suggestively on the reins, he continued to back away and at length the horse followed, its flanks scraping against the rock wall to its left. It tried to shy away from it, then halted again, trembling violently. He patted its neck, keeping a hold of the reins in his right hand. There was a cold, clammy wetness on his forehead and the back of his neck. He could taste salt on his lips as he ran his tongue around them.

Speaking gently all the time, he inched along the break. Once, the horse's foot scraped the lip of the ledge at its narrowest point. It shifted its feet violently in an effort to retain its balance, then came forward with a rush, carrying him with it, coming to rest on safe, firm ground.

Taking off his hat, he rubbed his wet forehead. He felt hot and cold all at once. 'All right,' he called into the darkness. 'You can start comin' over, Menderer.' He moved further from the break, reached a point where there was a clear, wide patch of ground, moonlit, dotted with clumps of vegetation and waited there for the others to cross. He felt tired, hungry, and not a little apprehensive. They were taking too long and making too much noise. Now that the storm had passed into the distance, any sound they made would carry well. Off in the night fresh sounds rose and lifted and as he sat there, staring about him, he tried to identify them, but failed. Very often, they were only broken fragments of sound which lacked definition.

He was still listening when Menderer came up to him, leading his mount. The other's face was shiny with sweat in the flooding moonlight. He said softly, hoarsely: 'I wouldn't like to have to go through that again for all the gold these *hombres* got away with. If this is the only way down this side of the mountains, I vote we go on over the summit and down the other side of the range.'

'You may have somethin' in that,' Clint affirmed. They waited for the others to come up, one by one, their faces tight.

Roderick pushed his mount up to Clint's. 'We made that easier than I'd expected. The trail should be good for the rest of the way to the mine.'

'How far to the Turral mine now?' Clint asked sharply.

' 'Bout two miles,' nodded the other. He lifted a hand and pointed up into the moonlight. 'There are a couple of shacks on either side of the trail before you get to the mine workings proper. They used 'em for the assaying. Then the vats that held the cyanide liquor. My guess is they could have a couple of men in the assay shacks, or on top of one of the vats. From there, they'd be able to watch the trail for a mile or more. Even in this moonlight. It's bright enough for 'em to pick out a file of men.'

Clint reached a sudden decision. 'We'll ride on for half a mile, then go the rest of the way on foot,' he ordered. 'That way, we can move through the brush borderin' the trail, keeping under cover most of the way.'

Menderer nodded, but said nothing. It was impossible to tell anything from his shadowed face. With Roderick leading the way, they moved forward along the upgrade trail once more.

SEVEN
Outlaw Justice

Standing near the window of the small cabin close to the gaping mouth of the old mine workings, the Matagorda Kid was able to see most of the way down the slope. The moonlight, slanting across it, threw long, irregular shadows among the rocks and the gravel piles which lifted in smoothly rounded humps at intervals along the wide trail. Just beyond the last of them he could clearly see the tall cyanide vats on their wooden piles, lifting their bulk high above the ground. Haig Calton was somewhere on top of one of them where he could see any oncoming riders quite clearly. Further away, in the assay shacks which stood at the very entrance to the mine workings, almost a quarter of a mile down the trail, Levin and Bulmer were keeping watch.

Inwardly, he felt worried, although he had tried not to show it to the others. By now, Fleck should have reached this place. Even if his horse had gone lame on him and he had been forced to pick the easier, although the more roundabout, trails, it was still too long. More than ever, he felt certain that something had happened to the other and the thought was a nagging, frustrating feeling at the forefront of his mind. He recalled the bunch of cowpokes where they had shared camp before riding up into the hills. Then he dismissed the immediate thought. They had not been suspicious of them; he felt sure of that and there had been no reason for any of those men to ride into the hills on their trail and eventually catch up with Fleck. Yet something had happened to him and he could not get the feeling out of his mind that Fleck had been either killed or captured by the law. Dead, and Fleck was no problem. But if he had been taken alive by a posse riding out from Vendado, then he may have talked, may have told the lawmen in the town where they were.

'You look like a man with somethin' on his mind,' said Weller from the table in the middle of the hut. 'Quit worryin' about Fleck. If you want my opinion, he's decided to pull out while the goin' was good. By now, he'll be fifty miles across the Mexico border and you won't see his heels for dust.'

The Kid shook his head slowly, but emphatically. 'He wouldn't go without takin' his share of the loot from that train,' he said harshly. 'You know Fleck as well as I do. He'd come here for his share even if he had to walk every step of the way.'

'Then what do you figure happened?' The other did not look up, but thumbed the pack of greasy cards, shuffling them slowly.

'I figure that somebody rode out from Vendado and found our trail at that point where we killed those three men, then followed it across to that line camp. Those cowpokes there would have told him about us, you can be certain of that. They'd even have mentioned about Fleck havin' a crippled mount.'

'So they trailed him instead of us and took him back into Vendado.'

'I guess that's it. And whether he wanted to or not, he'll have talked by now.'

Weller pushed back his chair, walked over to the window, glancing out into the flooding moonlight. He was silent for a long moment, then he said meaningly: 'From here a man can see more'n five hundred yards. With a

Winchester I reckon he could pick off a man before he could get into a position to fire back.'

The Kid grinned 'Just what I was thinkin'. That's why I've got the others down there to keep an eye on the trail.'

Weller pursed his lips tightly for a moment in thought. 'You think it likely they'll tackle that trail in the dark? It's a helluva track even in full daylight.'

'They'll try it, even if only to take us by surprise. They probably figure that this is the one way we won't be expectin' them to come.'

Weller did not look up. He was studying the cigarette he had just rolled, a match in his other hand. Lighting it, he watched the smoke curl up from the tip of it.

'This place is like a fortress. We can hold off an army here if we play our cards right.'

'Fact is though that they managed to find that other hide-out of ours and kill Sunter. Lucky we didn't have the money hidden there or that would have gone.'

The Kid nodded. He knew what was coming next, knew that Weller was one of the band who was beginning to get scared now that he could feel the net closing in a little around them.

'Kid, why don't we just share out the dough and head for the border while we still have the chance. There'll be lawmen swarming all over the territory soon because of that robbery. Pinkerton men, troopers, posses. We won't have a chance. But in Mexico we'd be safe. Reckon there ain't no sense in hangin' on to that money until we're all in jail or shot to pieces.'

'Now you're talkin' like a scared fool,' said the Kid harshly. 'Like I said before, we got to share that among nearly twenty men. It won't mean much for each of us. Besides, if we can lie low for a week or so, they'll figure that we did head for the border and the heat will soon be off here. Then we can start again.'

'You're not being reasonable.'

'You do as I say,' murmured the other, his tone soft, but

threatening. 'I give the orders and I say that we sit tight until they quit lookin' for us in this neck of the woods. Just so long as we keep calm, everythin' will turn out all right. But I'm not goin' to have anybody runnin' off.' He saw the change in expression on the other's face as the flare of the tip of the cigarette touched his features with orange light as he inhaled sharply. 'We're in this together now. I can bring us all through this without trouble, but I need obedience to do it. Complete obedience, you understand?'

'Sure. Sure I understand, Kid.' Weller nodded his head quickly. His adam's apple bobbed up and down rapidly.

'Good. I sometimes get the idea that you don't like it here with the rest of us. Since Fleck didn't show up, I get the feelin' you'd like to cut and run for it, maybe turn yourself over to that sheriff's posse. Could be that you think you'll escape the noose if you tell them everythin' you know.'

'Listen, Kid, I wasn't thinkin' anything of the kind,' muttered the other defensively. His glance went down the slope and suddenly, he stiffened, pointed.

The Kid peered in the direction of the other's pointing finger. The figure on top of the cyanide vat had risen on to its knees. He could see Calton quite clearly in the moonlight. The other was waving his arm quickly in a warning signal.

'Somethin's wrong,' he snapped harshly. 'Stay here with the others until I check. If anythin' happens down there, be ready to give me coverin' fire.' He spoke to Weller, but his words were addressed to the other men in the hut. Stepping outside, into the cold night air that swept down the side of the hill, he walked quickly down the track towards the vats, feet sliding on the loose shale. The horses were kept saddled just inside one of the mine shafts that led into the depths of the hill. He heard them moving restlessly in the darkness as he moved down the slope.

There was a narrow wooden ladder leading from the ground, up past the stout wooden struts which supported the main structure, and past the side of the vat itself. For a moment, he paused in the moon-thrown shadow of the structure, stared up but could make out nothing of Calton and not wanting to risk calling out, he began to climb the ladder. He had made himself calm and now he sucked air down into his lungs. breathing slowly and regularly until he reached the top, stared out at Calton.

'They're coming,' said the other hoarsely. He wriggled forward, balancing himself carefully on the top of the vat. The thick wooden lid was splintered in places, did not look too safe to the Kid's trained eyes and he remained where he was, legs braced on the topmost rung of the ladder, leaning his weight on his elbows as he stared down towards the scrub that bordered the trail, where it led off as a pale grey scar down the steep hillside. He could just make out the small assay shacks, hemming in the trail. There was no sign of the two men in them.

'I don't see anythin',' he said finally, shading his eyes against the glare of the moonlight. 'You sure you saw somethin'?'

'Certain. I don't make mistakes like that.'

'Were they on horseback?'

'Nope. I caught a glimpse of two of 'em running through that scrub oak just beyond the bend in the trail. They were carryin' Winchesters by the look of it.'

The Kid eyed that portion of the trail musingly, through narrowed eyes. He appeared to have misjudged the sheriff from Vendado and his posse. Somehow, they must have got hold of one of the prospectors who knew every trail there was in these hills. That was the only way they could have found their way up here in so short a time – for he was positive now that Fleck had been taken alive and forced to tell all he knew – maybe with the promise of a lesser sentence once the whole band had been brought to justice. His lips curled back over his teeth in a derisive, sneering smile. Well, whoever they were and no matter how many men this sheriff had at his back, they would soon discover that they had bitten off more than they could chew when they had decided to ride out and attack him here.

A moment later, he glimpsed the running figure that darted from one concealing shadow, across an open stretch of ground, throwing itself down behind a clump of mesquite. He sucked in a sharp breath, then nodded.

'You were right, Haig,' he said softly. 'Here they come. Wait until they get closer before you open fire. If those other two down there have any sense they'll let most of those men get past them, wait for us to open up, and then let them have it from behind when they try to make their way back.'

'Not much chance of that,' grated Calton thinly. 'Levin and Bulmer are both men with itchy trigger fingers. They'll start shootin' as soon as they spot any of those *hombres.*'

The next moment, the sharp bark of a rifle shattered the clinging stillness. The echoes chased themselves flatly among the rocks and boulders. The bullet did not find its mark, but it brought a crashing volley of return fire from the men hiding among the mesquite bushes and scrub oak less than a hundred feet from the two assay shacks.

'Now they've stirred up a goddamned hornet's nest,' muttered the Kid through his tightly clenched teeth. 'But maybe they can hold them off down there for a while. They've got plenty of cover.'

'You want me to stick around here?' queried the other. He spoke low and even and if there was any fear in his mind, he did his best not to show it.

'Just keep your eyes open, wait until any of them try to slip past the shacks. We'll back you up with covering fire when you make a break for the mine. They've got to head up this trail now that they've decided to move in from that direction.' He threw a quick glance at the tall, spired peaks that towered around them, rearing up to the moon-lit heavens. At least, those men down there would not be able to climb them and take them from the flanks. He smiled grimly to himself as he went down the ladder hand over hand, dropped the last half dozen feet to land lightly on his toes. Swiftly, he raced back up the shale slope to the cabin.

He was less than five feet from the door of the cabin when it burst open. He caught a glimpse of Weller running out, grim features shiny in the moonlight. Even before he could divine the other's intentions, there came a startled shout from inside the hut, distracting his attention from the man in front of him for a fraction of a second. But it was long enough for Weller to swing a haymaker at his jaw, with all of the wiry weight and strength of the other behind the blow. Desperately, acting purely on instinct, he tried to ride the blow, turning his head and ducking under it. But he was not quite quick enough. The other's hard-bunched knuckles caught him a glancing blow on the point of the jaw, knocking him backward. He hit the ground hard, lay with all of the wind knocked out of his lungs, gasping for breath. He saw the other continue to run down the hillside, scuffing at the shale and stones with his boots, arms and legs flailing wildly as he strove to keep his balance.

Cleaver came rushing out of the hut, lifted his arm and aimed the Colt after the fleeing man. His face was twisted into a mask of anger and there was a bloody streak down one cheek. He loosed off a couple of shots after the other, the bullets kicking up the rocks around the other's running feet.

There came a single gun flash from the top of the cyanide vat as Haig opened up. By now, Weller was almost level with the vat, had swerved violently to one side as his mind registered the presence of this new danger. Another shot from Calton and Weller staggered, fell on to his hands and knees, rolled several feet down the slope, his body temporarily lost in the black shadow of the vat. Then he got to his feet again, continued to run, swaying drunkenly from side to side, crashing through the tall scrub that grew along the sides of the trail. He reached the bend near the assay huts, swerved off once more and was lost to sight.

Cleaver cursed loudly under his breath. Thrusting the Colt back into leather, he rubbed his fingers down his cheek for a moment, then seemed to recollect that the Kid was still lying dazed on the rocks. He came forward, bent and helped the other into the hut as a fresh round of firing burst out down near the bottom of the trail.

Lowering the Kid into the chair at the table, Cleaver said tightly: 'I ought to have shot him down earlier. I figured he was on the point of tryin' somethin' like that but it wasn't until he suddenly lunged for the door that I was sure. I guess I was a little slow.'

The Kid nodded. He felt his jaw tenderly. There was a momentary bubbling anger inside him, but he forced it down swiftly. What was done, was done; and there was nothing they could do about it now. Weller had been hit by Calton, there was no doubt about that and maybe he had been hurt bad, so that he would not be able to talk to those lawmen down there and even if he did, he would not live to profit by it.

'How many men are there down there?' Cleaver asked after a while, when the Kid got up and stood swaying groggily on his feet.

'Plenty,' muttered the other harshly. 'But we can take 'em without too much trouble. They can only come along the trail out yonder. It would take 'em far too long to try to move around us and take us from the sides, even if they dared to take a chance with those slopes yonder. We can keep 'em pinned down for an eternity.' He forced a ring of confidence into his tone.

'We can't stay for ever,' put in Cleaver softly.

'Why not?'

The other shrugged, knew that he was on dangerous ground with the Kid in his present angry mood, but also knowing that this was something which had to be said. 'Kid, there's only enough food here for two, maybe three, days and water for less. There ain't been a supply of water to this place for more'n fifteen years. You got to face facts.'

'You suggestin' then that we should give ourselves up to that posse out there in the hope they'd forget the robbery and those three men who were killed? They wouldn't even wait to get us to Vendado. They'd string us up from those trees out yonder.'

'I'm facing facts,' said Cleaver stubbornly.

'Facts don't mean a thing,' snapped the Kid thinly. 'You can always find a way around 'em if you look hard enough and long enough.'

'Maybe so. But we don't have that much time. It ain't easy to fight off a bunch of men like those with empty bellies and parched throats. I know how it was durin' the war. I've seen men surrenderin' just to get a drink of water, or a bite to eat.'

'You figurin' on tryin' to go the same way as that coward Weller?' said the Kid ominously.

Cleaver's head jerked up. For a moment he stared directly at the other. Then his gaze dropped, he shuffled his feet nervously on the floor of the hut. He said nothing, but after a moment's pause, the Kid went on tautly. 'I thought not. You'd never make it to the vats.'

Crouched down among the trees, holding the Winchester tightly in his right hand, Menderer only a few feet away, Clint McCorg peered up into the weirdly fantastic shadows that lay stretched among the rocks and across the wide trail. Far off, almost hidden by the sharply-angled bend in the trail, some fifty yards away, he could just make out the gaping hole of the mine shaft that led deep into the side of the hill and some sort of structure just beside it which he took to be the shape of the cabin where he figured most of the outlaws to be holed up. The assay huts that Roderick had mentioned were only a short distance away and he eyed them carefully, watching for any sign of life there. It was not likely that the Matagorda Kid would have been foolish enough to have overlooked the chance of a posse moving along this trail and the chances were that he had placed men in those huts as lookouts.

Glancing back, he waved two of the men forward, switched his gaze back to the shacks as the men ran over the rough, uneven ground, bodies bent low to present more difficult targets to anyone in the low wooden buildings. The first man dived for cover, went down behind one of the mesquite bushes on the far side of the trail. The second started forward and in that instant, a rifle cracked from one of the windows. Clint saw the stabbing muzzle flash in the darkness, lifted his own weapon and squeezed the trigger. The Winchester bucked against his wrist and he heard the bullet tear a splinter of wood from the window frame. The rest of the men poured a crashing, volley into the huts, adding their weight of fire to his and in the midst of all the noise and echoes, he heard a man give up a high-pitched yell of agony and then silence.

He gazed off up the slope, gauged the distance to the cyanide vats. They, too, would make an excellent vantage point, he thought reflectively. Even as he stared into the moonlight, he thought he saw a shadow move down the side of one of the huge wooden structures and run-off along the slope, heading back in the direction of the but near the workings. Beside him, Menderer had seen the man too and he lifted his rifle, squinting along the sights to draw a bead on the back of the fleeing man, but Clint touched his arm, tightening his grip a little.

'He's well out of range,' he whispered sharply. 'No sense in wastin' a bullet on him.'

Menderer relaxed, towered the rifle. 'I think we got that *hombre* in the nearer shack,' he observed. He was on the point of saying something further, when he paused, eyes widening a little. 'Look! There along the trail,' he said tensely. 'Somebody runnin' from the far shack.

Headin' down the slope like a madman.'

Clint narrowed his eyes, then nodded as he picked out the running, sliding figure of the man who came racing down the slope, legs pounding wildly as he strove to maintain his balance on the steep, uneven slope. There came the unmistakable crack of a Colt in the distance. Clint saw the running man begin to swerve and weave frantically from side to side, knew that the rest of the men in the but were firing at him.

'Looks like one of 'em didn't relish the idea of fightin' it out and he wants to give himself up,' said Menderer harshly.

'And it also appears that his friends don't want him to reach us alive,' Clint put in. 'If there is a man up on one of those vats, he'll pick him off as he gets nearer.' He sighted his Winchester on one of the vats, squinting through the Vee notch, made out the faint movement on the wooden cover of the structure and squeezed off a couple of shots to force the other to keep his head down. Even so, he saw the running man stagger as though he had been hit the moment before he ran into the shadow of the vat. Moments later, he came into view again, staggering now from side to side, one hand clutching at his shoulder. Abruptly, he veered off into the bushes on the side of the trail, was lost to sight and it was impossible to tell if he had fallen and was lying badly hurt in the brush, or if he was keeping out of sight until a better moment arrived to go the rest of the way.

'Keep me covered,' Clint snapped to Menderer. 'I'm goin' out there to bring that *hombre* in.'

Without waiting for the other to answer, he slid forward through the scrub, wriggling along the ground on his belly. He had left the Winchester behind and, unhampered by it, he went even lower, pressed his body flat upon the ground to inch forward around the second assay hut, exposing only a small part of his body. He felt sure that one man had been killed during the firing earlier, but there could be another man crouched inside this shack, keeping his eyes open, ready to fire the moment he caught sight of anything that moved in the moonlight.

There was, some distance ahead, between shack and a small knot of trees, a pile of logs, evidently cut some time before against the day when whoever had owned the mine built a corral for the horses and burros they had. Now they would provide Clint with the cover he needed.

Cautiously, he worked his way towards them, lay crouched behind them for several seconds, listening to the occasional crack of rifle fire in the distance, then gathered his legs under him, took several deep breaths, and then hurled himself forward, head down, rushing towards the trees. Immediately, a gunshot from behind, shattered the temporary silence and he heard the vicious hum of a bullet passing through the air close to his head. Then he was among the trees and the second slug sliced brown bark off one of them and sent a large sliver skimming through the air. Another shot came, but by then Clint was moving clear in anticipation and before still another shot came, he was deep among the trees that grew right up to the sheer face of the rock which hemmed in the trail at this point, searching around for the man he had seen run into the brush.

Seconds dragged past on leaden feet. Was it around here that the man had disappeared? The more he looked about him, the more dubious he was as to his position relative to the spot where he had seen the other stumble out of sight. Then he heard the faint rustle in the undergrowth, edged forward cautiously, telling himself that the other probably still had a gun and might use it to protect himself.

A moment later, he saw the other lying in the mesquite. The man was trying to push himself up on to his hands and knees. He was breathing heavily and his face, bloodless and grey with dust, bore an agonised expression, lips drawn back over his bared teeth. He held a Colt in one hand and tried to lift it feebly as he saw Clint moving towards him, then he lowered it reluctantly, as if lacking the strength to hold it lined up on the other. His eyes widened a little as Clint went down on one knee beside him and the sheriff's star, gleaming in the faint light, was visible for a moment as his jacket fell open.

'I'm givin' myself up,' gasped the other. 'I'm through with the others.'

'Throw away that gun,' Clint ordered. He waited until the other had complied, then bent and helped him to his feet. There was the warm slickness of blood on the front of the other's shirt, oozing from the wound high up in the shoulder. 'What's your name?' he asked sharply.

The other swayed, would have fallen but for the sheriff's restraining grip on his arm.

'Weller. Cal Weller. It was Haig Calton who tried to kill me. He's up on one of the cyanide vats, ready to pick you off as soon as you try to go forward. And they have two other men in the assay shacks.'

'I reckon we've killed one of them, probably the other,' Clint told him. 'What about the rest. Where are they holed up? In the cabin near the mine workings?'

'That's right.' The other swallowed, his tone hoarse and thick with the effort of speaking. 'They can cover the entrance into the workings for nearly two or three hundred yards, far enough to pick you off with Winchesters. It won't be easy to smoke 'em out of there.'

'What about food, water and ammunition?' asked Clint shrewdly.

The other forced a faint grin. 'You don't miss a thing, do you?' he murmured,. 'They got enough for perhaps two, three days. That's all.'

'That's what I figured.' Clint nodded, satisfied. He did not feel that the other was lying. Events had tended to show that he would tell the truth. Why he had run like that, risked his life to get to them and give himself up, he wasn't sure. Maybe he didn't want to hang with the rest of his former companions and believed that by taking this course, he would escape that fate. Maybe he was a coward and did not relish fighting, when the odds were against him. Or perhaps he had fallen out with the Matagorda Kid and decided to pull out while he had the chance.

But the news about the food and water was encouraging. He had feared that there might be a supply of water into the mine itself, left intact from the old days. Evidently there wasn't.

'I'll get you down to the others,' he said quietly. 'Then we'll take a look at that wound of yours. It looks worse than it really is. I figure the bullet is lodged up near the shoulder bone but it's too high to have touched the lung. Trouble is you're losin' blood. We've got to stop that bleedin'.'

He helped the other down the slope, keeping to the trees as far as possible and within ten minutes had rejoined Menderer and the others. By now, most of the men were in position around the two assay huts, ready to pour a withering hail of fire into the flimsy woodwork. Already, the wood around the door and the window of the nearer hut showed signs of the scarring caused by the earlier hail of fire.

'How bad is he?' Menderer jerked a thumb in the direction of Weller, who had been laid out on the ground some twenty feet back along the trail.

'Shot in the shoulder. Pretty high up. Reckon it's probably missed the lung, but hit the bone and there's been bleeding. Sooner he gets to a doc, the better his chances will be.' He deliberately kept his voice low so as not to be overhead by the wounded outlaw.

'Did he tell you anythin'?'

'There's ten or fifteen of 'em in the hut near the entrance. One on top of the vats and one in each of these huts. It's the Matagorda Kid all right. This time we've got him bottled up so tight he doesn't have a chance in hell of getting out of the trap. What's more important, they have only enough food and water for three days at the most.'

Menderer grinned. 'Things are soundin' better and better all the time,' he said softly. 'All we got to do is sit here twiddlin' our thumbs and makin' sure they don't come sneakin' down the trail, and they have to give up or die of hunger and thirst.'

'Could be. But I wouldn't underestimate the Matagorda Kid. There have been too many occasions in the past when a posse had him cornered and he still managed to slip out of the net. He won't give up that easy.'

'We might move up there and try to talk with him,' suggested one of the other men in a low tone. 'If he's sensible, he'll listen.'

Clint shook his head. 'He's wanted for murder now. So are most of the men with him. They know there's a rope waitin' for them at the end of the trail. Men with the shadow of the noose hangin' over them don't give up that easy. You can take my word for it, they'll fight to the last man and the last bullet.'

The man's eyes remained on the assay shack. Even as he watched, there came the vivid orange muzzle flash and a bullet struck close to their position.

Clint's men were ready. A savage fire poured into the shacks from all sides. They kept it up while two men made crude torches with dried grass wound tightly around the ends of thick sticks, lit them and crouching down, crawled forward to toss them through the windows. There came a harsh yell from inside one of the huts, but only silence from the other. Either the man there had been killed or he was so badly wounded he could not shout out or move.

The wood of which the huts were constructed was as dry as tinder. Long years of standing in the fierce sun had bleached all of the moisture out of the warped boards and even the brief storm of that night had not wetted them sufficiently to make any difference. Within seconds, they were beginning to burn furiously, with black smoke pouring out of the windows, lifting high into the still air.

Clint lay on his stomach, cradling the rifle in his hands, watching the doors of the two buildings, ready in case either man decided to run out into the open and fight it out. But for a long moment, there was no movement in the deep shadows. The flames leapt up and caught at the tarred roof of the nearer hut. Scarcely fifteen seconds later, it crashed in with a thunderous roar, sending up a shower of red sparks high into the air where they drifted lazily on the faint breeze before winking out.

There was no hope for the man in that building – probably, thought Clint, he had been dead anyway before the torch had been hurled in through the window. He recalled the harsh yell he had heard in the middle of the racket of that first volley, knew he was right. Even as the thought flashed through his mind, a dark figure appeared in the doorway of the second shack, his body outlined against the glare of the flames behind him. His clothing was alight, but he still held two Colts in his hands and as he staggered forward, he fired into the scrub, his bullets seeking out targets.

Clint yelled: 'Get him!'

Gunfire barked all around him. The man staggered, held himself up right by sheer iron will, loosed off two more shots, but already he was falling and they ploughed into the shale at his feet as he toppled forward, crashing on to his face in the dirt.

Menderer grumbled something under his breath. Clint turned. 'What was that?' he asked.

'I just said that we all have a clear conscience, even after that. We did our best to get them out with their hands lifted. It was their decision to stay and fight it out. Now what do we do?'

'Now we sit back and wait for the Matagorda Kid to make his next move,' said Clint. 'It might be a long wait.'

They moved a little further up the trail, the men watching the burning shacks out of the corners of their eyes as though unable to remove their gaze from them, or from the crumpled body that lay just in front of one of the smouldering buildings. Now and then, a little gust of stray breeze would bring the smoke over the ground into their nostrils and they would wrinkle their faces as it went down their throats, stinging and choking.

The night passed slowly. The disc of the moon drifted over the arch of the heavens. dipped westward and dimmed gradually against the increasing dawn light that spread itself across the eastern heavens, shaming the stars, dimming their radiance. Five o'clock passed. Six o'clock. A deep and pendant silence lay over everything now. It was difficult to believe that some of the most dangerous outlaws in this part of the territory were holed up less than a quarter of a mile away, determined to sell their lives dearly.

By sun-up, the silence was beginning to tell on most of their nerves. A small group played poker in a tiny clearing with a well-thumbed pack of cards, occasionally halting their play to throw quick, apprehensive glances in the direction of the cyanide vats and beyond them the small square cabin where they knew most of the outlaws were at that moment, probably watching them in turn.

Clint sat beside Menderer and Roderick. After a long pause, he said: 'You sure there ain't no other way up to that shack, Roderick? No way to get around the vats and take these critters from the rear without warnin'?'

'You can see that for yourself,' said the other harshly, making a sweeping movement with his right arm. 'If you try to move back and then come over the tops of those peaks, chances are you'd fall over the lip of the plateau before you got anywhere near the top. There's nary a handhold or a foothold in that solid rock. I've seen it for myself and I know what I'm talkin' about.'

'Could be you didn't look none too close,' said Clint. 'Especially if you weren't lookin' for a way up.'

'Wouldn't bank on that.' The other shook his head. 'Those critters yonder know they can hold you off until their supplies run out. Maybe they're hopin' on figurin' out somethin' before then.'

'Is there any other way out through the mine workings themselves?', put in the deputy. 'I've been sittin' here thinking about why the Kid allowed himself to be holed up here so short of supplies. Seems to me they've got their horses stashed away inside the tunnel and that could mean they have another way out.'

'Could be at that, I reckon,' mused the other. 'But I ain't never heard of one.'

'What's on your mind, Sheriff?' asked Menderer tautly. 'You thinkin' that maybe we ought to attack them before we starve them out?'

'I'm inclinin' that way,' affirmed the other. He lit a cigarette, drew the smoke deeply into his lungs, felt it take away most of the night coldness from his chest He eyed the distant hut thoughtfully, tried to push his gaze into the gaping black mouth of the mine itself, a yawning mouth in the side of the rocks. It was the only place where they could possibly put up their mounts, he told himself. Yet why hide them there unless there was another way out? The Kid was much too smart to allow himself to be run into a trap such as this. He had known all along that Fleck had been taken alive, that he would have talked. That was why he had stationed those three men along the trail leading up to the mine, to keep a close watch on this trail because he had known they would be coming for him and that this was the way they would come. Inwardly, he felt a vague sense of grudging admiration for the Matagorda Kid, for the way in which he had planned everything. Maybe if it had not been for the unwarranted killing of those three men, things might have been a little different. As far as he knew, the Kid had not killed before.

Stretching himself, lifting his arms above his head, he flexed the muscles of his shoulders, then ducked sharply, instinctively, as a rifle barked from the top of the nearby vat and a bullet shredded leaves from the branch just above his head. He swore softly to himself for having forgotten about that marksman crouched up there.

'That was a bit too close,' he said through his teeth. 'My own fault too for havin' forgotten about him.'

The peaks of the hills were now touched with a deep crimson as the sun rose higher. But most of the valley that lay spread out far below them, the valley across which they had ridden the previous evening lay in deep shadow, the hills looming over it, shutting off the sunlight.

It was not an easy thing to make up his mind what was the best thing to do in the circumstances. Certainly a frontal attack on those mine workings would be a costly business, even if they did succeed in the end, and he was not the sort of man willing to achieve his goal at any cost. But he had the feeling that he had been manoeuvred into a position where it was almost impossible to make any decision which would eventually turn out to be the right one.

At last, he said quietly: 'We'll have to split our forces if we want to take them quickly.' He shrugged. 'I'm leavin' you here with most of the men and taking only half a dozen myself.'

'What do you mean to do, Clint?' asked the other with a lift of his bushy brows. 'You got somethin' in mind?'

'I'm goin' to see if there ain't a way up the rear side of those rocks yonder, that could bring us out right behind the hut.'

'Roderick reckons there's no way up,' pointed out the deputy in a serious tone.

'I know. It's only a chance, but we have to do somethin' to force the issue with these men, make them show their hands before they're really ready to do so. That's the way to turn this situation to our advantage. Besides, I want to be sure I can cut off their retreat into the mine workings, just in case there is another way out through the mountain.'

EIGHT
Under the Gun

Events soon made it clear to McCorg why the Matagorda Kid considered himself to be safe inside the shack at the entrance to the Turral mine workings. Half an hour after leaving the rest of the men to watch the trail down the hillside, he crossed a small creek that ran swiftly down the sheer drop in a plummeting waterfall, sparkling and glittering in the sunlight, and looked up at the sheer wall of rock which faced him. Turning, he glanced at the faces of the men with him, could read their thoughts from the expressions on their sweat-shiny features and in their eyes as they turned their heads to look directly at him.

'Even a goat couldn't climb that,' said one of them gruffly. 'Clem Roderick was right. Not a handhold at all.'

Clint said nothing, but angled his way thoughtfully to one side, splashing back through the rushing water of the creek, eyes not missing anything. At last, he found what he had begun to suspect. Over the years, perhaps the centuries, the stream had gouged a channel through the rock, a channel that twisted its way up to almost the topmost point above their heads. He pointed. 'There's the way to the top,' he said harshly.

Costello squinted up into the sunlight reflected off the rock. Here and there it glittered with crystals of quartz and other minerals, a variety of colours that dazzled the eye.

141

He shook his head. 'Even that isn't possible, Sheriff.'

Clint pressed his lips tightly together, screwing up his eyes. It was not going to be easy, he was sure of that, but on the face of it, he considered it to be possible. Anyway, he told himself, it was their only chance. Going forward, he began to climb, the ice-cold water splashing over his legs as he hauled himself up. He was forced to stop many times to get his wind and to ease the almost numbing, intolerable ache in his arms and legs. Slowly, he inched up the cliff face. Movement was a mechanical thing, an endless-seeming rhythm, from weariness to movement, from movement to a hauling, dragging motion and back to weariness again. How long he pulled himself up that channel with the water thrusting against him, it was impossible to tell. But then, when he thought it would be out of the question for him to go any further, he realized that the rocks were no longer above his head but on a level with him, that he had done it and was now at the top!

Unfastening the long, coiled riata from his belt, he made one end secure to an upthrusting rock, tested it, then let the rope snake down the rock face. Costello was the first to come up, pulling himself hand over hand up the rope which Clint had made fast to the pinnacle of rock. As he neared the top, Clint leaned down, grasped him by the wrists and hauled him up the rest of the way. For a long moment, the other lay on a flat outcrop of smooth stone, his mouth sagging open, his barrel chest heaving and wheezing with his laboured breathing. His eyes were narrowed almost to pinpoints, glazed a little with the exertion.

'Reckon you can help the others up, Costello,' McCorg said tightly. 'I'm goin' to scout out the position yonder.' He jerked a thumb in the direction of the rocky ledge which he knew, from what he had seen down below in the canyon, overlooked the mine workings and lay almost directly above and behind the shack where the outlaw gang were holed up.

Costello nodded his head slowly, pushed himself wearily to his feet and took Clint's place near the rope. Already, one of the other men was halfway up the sheer rock face, clinging with straining arms to the rope, holding himself off from the rocks with braced legs.

Crawling forward towards the ledge, Clint was half blinded by the white dust thrown into his face by the gusty wind that blew with an increasing force up here. His hardboned length hugged the rugged rocks behind a covering clump of huisache which miraculously grew out of the thin skin of dry soil covering the rock itself. A couple of feet from the edge, he paused. The dull overtones of voices reached him in snatches, flung up from below by the wind. He lay quite still for several seconds, holding his breath, not sure how far he was from the shack and where the men were. Straining to listen, he tried to separate fact from fantasy, knowing that the wind, too, was making low moaning sounds that were somehow blending with the murmur of conversation, so that it was impossible to make out the words.

Finally, he edged forward, moving by pulling himself over the rough surface of the ledge with his hands. The tricky overtones of shadow and the sighing breeze endowed the rocky ledges below him with movement in every direction. He lifted his head slowly, an inch at a time. The roof of the shack came into view a little off to one side, perhaps fifteen feet away from where he lay, between it and the rocky wall below him. He studied their faces closely. One he recognized, Art Cleaver, wanted for robbery, murder, and any other crimes which one could think of. A dangerous man, fast with a gun, ready to kill at the drop of a hat. Clint thinned his lips as he watched the men, knowing they had not seen him. It was odd, but at a time like this, the last direction a man ever thought of looking for danger, was up.

Very carefully, he slid sideways, moving closer to the

three men. At last, he could hear a little of what they were saying.

In a harsh tone, Cleaver said: 'First Fleck must've talked and now they'll have found Weller. He'll shoot off his mouth as soon as he gets to 'em.'

'Could be that Haig managed to hit him before he got down,' suggested one of the men.

'Mebbe so. But did he kill him? If he only wounded him, that posse will know we've got scarcely any water left. They'll stake themselves out at the bottom of the trail and we'll stay bottled up here until we either die of thirst or we're forced to give ourselves up.'

'You put this to the Kid?'

'Sure.' There was a note of bitter disgust in the other's voice that Clint noticed at once. 'He reckons he's got some plan for gettin' us out of here. My guess is that only the Matagorda Kid will get out. The rest of us will stay. That way, he gets all of the money and he won't have to worry about us. A fast horse and he could be across the Mexico border in a day. Then they'd never catch him.'

'Let's have it out with him right now,' grunted the tallest man tightly. 'He ain't runnin' this show if that's what he's got in his mind.' He hitched his gunbelt a little higher about his waist suggestively. They moved towards the side of the shack. For a moment, Clint's fingers tightened around the butt of one of the Colts at his waist, then forced himself to relax. It would have been so easy to get the drop on those three men, but that would have warned the others inside the shack and forced his hand.

The last of the three men moved out of sight around the edge of the shack and at the same instant, a volley of rifle fire cracked out down the slope. Bullets pecked at the dirt around the hut and some struck sharply against the wooden walls. There came the sound of muted yelling and the scuffle of feet as the three outlaws piled swiftly through the front door to get under cover. More yelling came from inside the shack followed by the savage bark of rifle fire.

Clint switched his gaze, peered down the trail. He could make out the man lying flat on top of the lid of one of the cyanide vats, firing steadily into the scrub at Menderer and the rest of the posse.

Then, abruptly, two men carrying smoking torches, ran from the scrub, converging on the vat from two sides. Feet pumping, they got beneath it before the man on top could bring his rifle to bear on either of them. The outlaw must have realized his danger, for he began edging back to the lip of the lid. Already, the stout wooden supports were beginning to flame, smoke lifting into the air. The crackling of the flames could be heard quite clearly even from where Clint lay.

From down below, a voice inside the shack yelled: 'Hell, they're tryin' to smoke Calton out.'

More gunfire roared out. Bullets kicked up dirt around the wooden supports of the vat. The two men crouched beneath them, their work done, waited for covering fire from the scrub, then ran in rapid spurts of movement for cover, bobbing and weaving from side to side as they ran.

Calton, balanced on top of the vat, almost totally obliterated by the thick, curling smoke, was firing savagely at the men in the brush, levering his rifle rapidly. Then, his rifle empty, he threw it away and edged back for the ladder. The orange-tongued flames, licking up from beneath the wooden structure were almost touching the vat itself now and Calton was halfway down the ladder when the weakened structure collapsed under his weight, pitching him heavily to the ground. For a moment, he lay there, with all of the air knocked from his lungs, one leg twisted strangely under him. Then, he somehow managed to push himself up on one arm, tug the pistol from his belt, and began firing defiantly into the trees and scrub. His body jerked spasmodically as bullets tore into it. For a moment, he remained upright, then sagged slowly to one side, sprawling out in the dust.

'That means the rest of the boys should be able to move

in closer to back us up,' whispered Costello.

Clint turned his head, saw the other crouched down beside him. The other five men were strung out near the ledge, waiting for him to give the signal to move in. A cloud passed in front of the sun and for a moment they crouched there in a cool shadow. Suddenly, a man in the shack below them was shouting harshly: 'They killed Calton. They're movin' up the slope.'

Clint got his legs under him, moved right to the edge of the ridge. It was a drop of nearly fifteen feet to the rocky floor of the canyon, but he noticed a narrow ledge, barely wide enough for a man, that led part of the way down the rock wall. He motioned with his hand for the others to follow, pointed at the ledge, then drew his gun and stepped out of cover. At that same moment, there was the sound of a door being kicked open and a small knot of men burst into sight at the side of the shack, keeping the building between themselves and the oncoming posse.

One of the men, turning his head sharply, glanced up, saw the group of men above him, swung his gun and yelled loudly. Clint fired from the hip and the man's shout broke off in the middle as he fell forward, clutching at his chest, the rifle falling from his nerveless fingers.

The others moved back out of sight behind the hut. But Clint knew that they were now forced to move quickly if they were to press home their advantage.

Legs slipping under him, he made the descent in five seconds, landed on his heels with a jarring impact that smashed clear up to the back of his skull. He fought to keep his balance, then ran forward, threw himself against the back of the shack, waved the others down. They came in a tight, scrambling bunch, their gushing breath harsh in their lungs.

'They're at the back of the hut, goddamnit!' yelled a voice.

Another voice shouted: 'Then fire through the wall, damn you. It's flimsy enough.'

Clint dropped on to his face with only a second to spare. Bullets splintered through the woodwork. Lead flailed through the wall. One of his men died before he had a chance to hit the ground. Clint heard death come to the other in a shocking, tearing sound as the lead ploughed through wood, then cloth, into flesh and bone. The man fell across Clint's legs, but there was no time for him to turn his head and see who it was. Crawling forward on his elbows, dragging his legs behind him, he moved around the corner of the shack, saw the three men who were racing hell for leather in the direction of the gaping hole in the side of the mountain.

'Get those men in the shack,' he yelled hoarsely. Getting to his feet, ignoring the whine of bullets that hammered about him, cutting through the air like a swarm of angry hornets, he raced after the three men, firing as he ran. He saw one of them throw up his arms, drop his gun, and pivot swiftly before collapsing in the dust. His hat fell from his head and cartwheeled over the rocks before coming to rest several feet from the man's body. Leaping over the dead man, Clint ran on without breaking his stride. The two outlaws were now less than twenty yards from the mining entrance and he felt a little sense of puzzlement. One of the men, even with his face turned from him, looked oddly familiar, the lithe gait, the easy movement, the shape of his head from the rear.

He loosed off another couple of shots, but both missed and a moment later, the two men had vanished inside the entrance, running between the rusted rails which led inside. Clint slowed to a walk, pressed himself tightly against the rocky entrance, gun in hand. There was no sound from inside the workings. Thumbing shells into the chambers of the gun, he reloaded it, hesitated for a moment, then plunged into the darkness inside the workings. Large boulders thrust themselves out from the walls of the tunnel and in front of him, it stretched forward into a well of inky blackness. He was acutely aware of the fact that he was outlined against the daylight that penetrated a few yards into the workings.

Keeping as close to the rocky wall as possible, he moved on cautiously, feeling in front of him with his left hand. Behind him, in the distance, the firing continued, a tremendous wave of sound which, channelled by the enclosing walls of the tunnel, vibrated and reverberated in his ears as he advanced into the darkness. He had a creepy feeling about his position. Those two men could be lying in wait for him anywhere in these workings, no doubt knew them much better than he did, would be watching for him, ready to pick him off the moment he gave himself away.

Suddenly, the wall under his hand slanted away from him, curving off to the left. Here, he paused. There was only a very vague, dim light here now and the mouth of the tunnel, some thirty yards away, yawned a glaring white against the shrouding blackness. Every muscle in his body was so tight with tension and suspense that they began to ache intolerably, and his thigh muscles were tight with cramp, pain lancing up into the lower half of his body. But his mind seemed strangely clear and it was as if he was able to pick out the smallest sounds as though they were magnified in some odd way. As he stood there, holding his breath until it hurt in his lungs, he heard the faint clatter of metal on metal, like a boot striking one of the rails which ran down into the bowels of the earth. It echoed hollowly from one side of the tunnel to the other, making it almost impossible to pick out its source.

Keeping well in to the side, he moved slowly forward again, straining all of his senses. The palm of his left hand came down on a jagged, upthrusting splinter of rock that pierced the flesh and he felt the warm slickness of blood on his skin. Wrapping his neckpiece around it, squeezing tightly on it, he peered into the velvet darkness. He could see nothing at all. Yet he had the unshakeable feeling that someone was there, waiting as he was, tensed and ready.

He let his breath fall away, advanced for another ten yards, then stopped abruptly. Someone was breathing heavily not far away and a second later, he heard the scrape of a man's body along the wall, judged the other to be on the other side of the tunnel and not more than ten yards away. Were both of the men there? he wondered; or had one of them moved on, leaving the other behind to lie in wait for him. He set one foot forward and down, testing the earth floor in front of him, moving the toe of his foot forward to feel for any loose rocks that might have been lying around. In his nostrils, there was the smell of the dust lifted by the two men. Three paces onward and the tips of his questing fingers touched a piece of board slanted up against the wall of the shaft. He came near it, felt it gently, and when it moved slightly under his touch, bringing dust down from the roof on top of his head, he went down swiftly and instinctively on one knee. The blue-crimson flash of gunfire lanced through the darkness, dazzling him and the bullet which had been intended for him, struck the rocky wall less than a foot away and whined off into the dark distance with a thin, high-pitched screech of tortured metal.

Even as the thunderous echoes died away and the smell of gunpowder assailed his nostrils, he had jerked up his own handgun, firing at the muzzle flash before the hidden gunman could step away. He heard a grunt as his bullet found its target in yielding flesh. Somebody scraped along the far wall, moving away, but not quickly as an unwounded man would, but slowly and hesitatingly, as if forced to cling to the outjutting rocks for support. The man's faint breathing was now a harsh, wheezing sound, that grated in the stillness.

Clint lifted his gun once more, then paused as he heard a fresh sound in the distance, deeper in the tunnel. It was an unmistakable sound. The whinney of a horse and hoof-beats moving away from him.

So there was another way out of the tunnel and the

other man had taken it, had left his companion to fight it
out alone. Sucking in a heavy gust of wind, Clint edged
forward, crossed the rails that thrust themselves up from
the ground, came to the far face of the tunnel and worked
his way cautiously along it towards the guttural breathing
of his unseen assailant.

Ten yards further on, and he almost stumbled over
something lying at his feet. Bending over the man, he
touched the other's body, shook him with his left hand,
felt the slackness that was in the man's limbs, listening for
his breathing but heard nothing, and let the other fall
back. There was no time to waste now. The other man and
he did not doubt that it would be the Matagorda Kid
himself, was getting away.

He moved quickly through the darkness and as he
walked, he realized that the air in his face was still fresh,
perhaps fresher than that near the mouth of the tunnel,
and it was blowing at him from dead ahead. This new
piece of information told him that the hidden entrance to
the tunnel was not far ahead. He saw the faint glow of
diffuse light as he rounded another bend in the tunnel
and came to a place where the tunnel widened. A couple
of brush torches had been thrust into brackets stuck into
the walls and he guessed that the outlaws used this part of
the workings regularly. Several boxes were strewn about
the tunnel and off to one side, there was a small bunch of
horses, tethered to iron rings in the wall.

He chose one of them, a long-legged animal that
looked as if it had plenty of speed and staying power about
it, tightened the cinch under its belly and swung up swiftly
into the saddle.

He rode straight into the darkness that opened off at
the far end of the open space, entered a narrower tunnel
along which cool air was blowing strongly, and let the
horse have its head. He felt restless, filled with an urgent
haste, yet knew better than to hurry his mount in this pitch
blackness. Gradually, the trail slanted downwards, began

to open out a little. He guessed that this part of the trail was not man-made, but was probably the dried-up watercourse of some ancient river which had flowed through the side of the mountain many ages before.

Ten minutes later, daylight showed ahead of him and he came out of the mountain, into a dense thicket of thorn and manzanita. There was a narrow trail winding into a belt of timber, then out again into a long valley that stretched down the hillside and into rougher ground perhaps two miles away. He screwed up his eyes to peer into the flooding sunlight which touched this side of the hills with a yellow radiance and a moment later, he saw the solitary rider who broke out of the timber and headed down into the valley, pushing his mount at breakneck speed. Once again, there was that nagging familiarity about the other, but Clint put it out of his mind as he touched spurs to his mount's flanks and urged it forward towards the trees.

The tall pines closed about him as he rode into them, ducking his head as one or two stray branches reached out, threatening to sweep him from the saddle as he passed beneath them. There was the aromatic smell of cones and needles in his nostrils and a green coolness under the closely-woven umbrella of twigs and leaves over his head, shutting out the sunlight, leaving only a pale green radiance that filtered down to the soft ground. There was an emptiness and a strangely suppressed quiet about the hills now, a warning that he felt bound to heed.

There was no sign of his quarry when he came out of the trees and started across the valley. A little later, he crossed another trail that wound up from the foothills, edging over a narrow crest and then up towards the summit. The horse frequently slowed and he had to continually urge it on, touching rowels to its flanks. Dust stayed with him to indicate that the other was still ahead of him. Whether the Matagorda Kid knew he was being pursued or not, was something Clint did not know. But the other was headed south, and might even be thinking of continuing all the way to Mexico. Certainly if he was carrying all of the loot with him, he would not stop until he was across the border and out of reach.

Half-way along the valley, with perhaps another mile to go before he reached the other end, he caught the sudden movement off to his left, turned his head sharply, then cursed himself for having been such a fool as to believe that his quarry would continue straight ahead if he knew he was being followed. Somehow, the other had doubled back, cut away from the trail and was at that very moment almost in the foothills, swinging out towards the prairie that stretched away to the desert between the hills and the distant Mexico border.

Swiftly, he swung his mount, brought down his spurs, sorry for the horse as he did so. It jumped into a dispirited run, plunged through the manzanita and Spanish bayonet grass that ripped cruelly at it, shying away as it tried to get out of the long, sword-like growth. Clint held it on to its trail with a tight hold on the reins. He looked anxiously to the shadowed ridges which ran parallel with the trail he had chosen, knew that he could not climb them, that he would have to hold to that he had chosen, and even so, it meant the other would have quite a lead on him once he did manage to reach the prairie. But that could not be helped. If he had had his wits about him and had realized the possibility of this, he might have spotted the other's move earlier.

Coming out of the foothills, with the sun now dropping lower from the zenith, Clint studied the terrain in front of him thoughtfully. He was slightly higher than the lone rider spurring across the prairie but he could just make out the other's position by the dust cloud thrown up by his mount.

As the afternoon turned into evening and the light began to seep away from the sky and surrounding country,

Clint McCorg gradually closed the distance between himself and the man he was trailing. He knew that he was taking a risk if he got too close, that the other would certainly turn and fight and would inevitably do so on ground of his own choosing. There was no chance of catching up with the Matagorda Kid before nightfall. The other had too great a lead on him and once it was dark, trailing him would be even more dicey than now. But the other was headed straight for the border, had shown no signs of slowing his pace or turning off the trail south, and he was gambling that he would stay that way.

After a few more miles, he left the grassy scrubland behind, rode out into the desert proper, dust drifting to him on the wind. He steadied his pace again, head bowed a little in the saddle as the irritating grains scoured his flesh and burned his eyeballs, working their way under his eyelids, half blinding him. Now that it was becoming dusk he had to be real careful. It was not likely that he would run into any stray riders out here. Unless they were running from the law, men avoided these Badlands like the plague. There was little water until one hit the far edge more than thirty miles away and the few waterholes there were, would in all probability be dried up now, after the long, hot spell. The small fume of dust that marked the position of his quarry was just visible in far distance, too far away for him to make out the shape of horse or rider, but enough to keep a watch on the man with fair certainty. The sun had set fifteen minutes before and there was still a narrow bar of crimson-gold stretched across the western horizon off to his right, with the wispy stain of dust hanging against it.

Sitting straighter in the saddle, he watched it for a long moment, running the tip of his tongue around his dry, parched lips. He felt like a drink, but knew there was only half a canteen of water in his waterbottle and no way of knowing when he would reach any more, so he bided his time, tried to put his mind on to something else, ignoring his thirst.

He rode into a narrow gully that wound between two high ridges of alkali, was out of sight of the other for several minutes. As he rode, he tried to assess the best course of action now that night was falling. If he was to keep a watch on the other he would be forced to close the distance even more and that increased the possibility of an ambush. On the other hand, if he dropped back a little so as not to arouse the other's suspicions, and hope to pick him up again at dawn, there was the chance he might lose him. He began to regret now that he had not signalled more of the men in the posse to follow him into the tunnel. Had there been more of them out here, they could have cut the Matagorda Kid off with ease in the dark, circling around him, trapping him in a narrowing circle. But one man alone, had to play things very carefully.

Making up his mind, he squeezed his horse's barrel with his legs, touched spurs to its flanks, urging it forward. Daylight now was no more than a pale grey memory in the west and the brilliant crimson stripe that had lain close to the horizon was almost dead. He rode cautiously, keeping up the rapid trot, eyes fixed on that spot of dustsmoke ahead of him.

The first stars began to gleam in the east and the feeling of anxiety in his mind increased. The thought of losing the other now that he had trailed him so far, now that he had smashed the outlaw gang and had only the leader himself to capture or kill. Kicking the horse into a flying gallop, he sent it racing headlong over the desert. His luck held. Long before the last trace of daylight had faded from the sky, he was less than half a mile from the other, could see him clearly now, urging his pony forward as rapidly as possible, in a cruel pace. Now it was a matter of which one had the horse with the most staying power. If the Matagorda Kid had had any sense, he would have chosen the best for himself, yet to Clint it seemed the other was slowing somewhat, that he was deliberately running his mount into the ground rather than trying to conserve its strength and energy.

Even as he rode on, there came a sudden bright wink of light from dead ahead and a muted crack whiffled past the side of his head as the bullet hummed close. Seconds later, he heard the vicious crack of the gun. He swerved, sent the horse wheeling to one side, then pulled it back towards the trail once more, his own gun out. Another slug murmured near him as he crouched low, urging the horse forward with his heels, riding like a madman over a rising ridge of sand. Thumbing the hammer of his pistol, he sent three more shots after the other. Almost at once, the other's horse staggered as it was hit by one of the bullets. Now the distance closed rapidly.

He saw the other leap from the saddle as the horse went down on to its knees, turn for a moment and then run for a cluster of rocks by the side of the trail. The other was gone from sight before Clint could fire the last two shots m his gun, and the lead screamed harmlessly off the top of the rocks. He reined up his mount quickly as gunfire erupted from in front of him, knew he would ride straight into it if he kept going. Now that he had the other pinned down, there was no sense in hurrying. He had plenty of time to finish this, once and for all.

Sliding from the saddle on the run, he dropped to the ground into a small gully that ran diagonally across the trail. The muzzle flashes of the Kid's gun glared briefly in the dark and lead screamed and cracked harshly all about him. Fragments of rock struck his cheek, brought blood as they sliced along his flesh. He ducked his head, crawled forward a few yards until he reached the end of the gully. Here, there was just sufficient cover for him if he lay flat and did not lift his head more than a few inches.

Now he felt more sure of himself, but he knew that it was a feeling he must not let get the better of him. The other was in an excellent strategic position. He breathed slowly, forcing himself to relax. Now we'll see how good this *hombre* is, he thought. Let the silence work on him for a little while and he'll begin to fire recklessly to cover his own apprehensive fear. All he had to do was wait the other out and sooner or later, the Matagorda Kid would make a mistake, and when he did, it would be his last.

Lying there on his stomach, Clint waited, staring off into the starlit, shimmering dimness. He could make out the rocks quite clearly now, humped shapes which stood up against the paler background of the sky and alkali desert. Here, the white alkali had a strange sheen all its own, giving some light to the surrounding terrain. With his elbows raising him just enough to see over the top of the gully, he let his gaze roam over the tumbled rocks. There was a bunch of mesquite close by and he knew that even if the other were looking directly at him it would not be easy for him to see him.

Sooner or later, the Matagorda Kid would do something definite. He was not the type to lie there all night without making some attempt, either to slide away into the background, or to get hold of Clint's horse which was the only means either of them had of getting out of this terrible wilderness. Once the sun rose the next day, the heat would become intolerable, sapping a man's strength as it brought all of the moisture out of his body.

'You still there, Marshal,' yelled the Kid suddenly.

Clint tightened his lips, felt a tiny shiver go through him. That voice! He tried to tell himself that he had made a mistake, that his mind was playing tricks with him, that after all these years he could not be sure of anything.

'I'm here,' he called back. 'Reckon you'd better give yourself up, Jed.'

There was a pause, a deep, clinging silence that began to eat at Clint's nerve.

'How'd you know my name?' For the first time, there was something more than derision in the other's tone, there was a perplexed bewilderment now and with a tensed, sinking feeling, Clint knew that he had been right. He was hunting his own brother.

'So it is you.' He almost forgot himself, lifting his head a little higher than he had intended. The bullet smacked against the hard dust an inch away and he flinched involuntarily as he pulled his head down, sucking air in through his teeth.

A moment later, he heard a harsh laugh from among the rocks, a sound that sent little tremors along his nerves. 'That ain't you, Clint, is it?'

'That's right. I never figured you for the Matagorda Kid.' He tried to keep the bitterness from his tone, but only partly succeeded. 'I don't want to have to kill you, but I'm takin' you in for the murder of those three men in Vendado. Better lift your hands where I can see them and walk out. I'll do my best for you when we get back to town. You got to realize that your days are finished. We've smashed your gang and without them, you're nothin'!'

'You finished, Clint?' sneered the other.

'I'm finished,' he muttered.

'Then you listen to me now. I've got close on three hundred thousand dollars here and I mean to keep it. Once I'm across that border and into Mexico you can't touch me.

'How do you figure on gettin' there, Jed? Your horse won't take you another step. A day on foot in this desert and you'll be mad. Better take the chance I'm offerin' you.'

'You've got it all wrong, brother. I'm a killer, remember? I've shot men down just for the sheer joy of killin'. But not you. I could drop you and not bat an eyelid because it's in me; but you wouldn't shoot me and even if you tried, you'd be slower.' He laughed harshly. 'I reckon you'll be the one staying here, Clint.' A pause, then the other went on: 'I'm comin' out now and if you try to stop me, I'll kill you. I mean that.'

A boot scraped on loose gravel. Clint moved quickly,

got his feet under him. He could picture Jed behind the rocks, still a little unsure of himself in spite of what he had said, but determined to go through with it. As he crouched there, waiting, he remembered the way in which his mother had died, how his father had followed her quickly to the grave.

It came suddenly. Almost before he was aware of it, Jed had got to his feet, was stalking forward, down the smooth rocks, moving towards the horse, standing patiently a few yards away. Clint had time to see that the other was carrying a heavy webbing bag in his left hand, his right clutching a Colt. Clint moved around the curve of the broad gully, said, sharply: 'Hold it right there, Jed. I don't want to have to kill you, but like I said, I will if you force me to.'

The other paused, not turning. He said sneeringly: 'You don't have it in you, Clint. You can't forget that I'm your brother, even if I am the Matagorda Kid, even if I am wanted for murder. Now move away and drop that gun, or I swear I'll let you have it.'

Clint shook his head slowly. 'I'm not goin' to let you get away with this, Jed, even if you are my brother. I'm sworn to uphold the law and if I were to give in now, it would make a mockery of everythin' I've tried to do since the citizens of Vendado elected me to this post.'

'You're a fool, Clint. I warned you that—' The other did not finish what he intended to say. It had all been a ruse to get Clint to concentrate on what he was saying rather than on what he meant to do.

He swung suddenly to face the other, a dimly seen figure in the shimmering starlight, bringing up the barrel of the Colt, lining it up on Clint's chest in a single, smooth movement, his finger tightening on the trigger.

A single shot bucketed out of the stillness. For a moment, Jed McCorg stood quite still, trying to hold the life in his eyes, eyes that widened just a little as they stared uncomprehendingly at the smoking Colt held firmly in Clint's hand. Slowly, his knees bent, the gun tilted from his lifeless fingers, the bag in his other hand crashed at his feet and he fell forward on to his face in the dust.

Clint went forward slowly, turned him over, looked down for what seemed an eternity into the dead face, noticing how all of the sneering lines of derision and stunned surprise seemed to have all been wiped away.

He buried his brother in the soft sand, placed a pile of rocks over the shallow grave, stood for a moment, then stooped to pick up the heavy bag, whistled up his horse and climbed wearily into the saddle. There was a strange emptiness in his mind which he could not understand. It was as if a part of him had died and been left behind there near that small knoll. The sighing wind cut keenly into his body and he shivered, pulled up the high collar of his jacket around his neck, turned away and rode back to the north.

Just before full dawn, he rode along the trail beside the foothills, met up with the posse working their way down from the high reaches of the hills. Menderer, sporting a bloody bandage around his arm, threw him a curious glance as he rode up to them, then stared down at the heavy bag tied to Clint's saddle.

'Did you catch up with the Matagorda Kid?' he asked quietly.

Clint nodded his head slowly. 'I found him,' he said dully. 'He was headed for the Mexico border with this.' He prodded the bag with his forefinger.

'Guess he never made it to the border, Sheriff,' called one of the men with a harsh laugh.

Clint stared at him unseeing for several moments, then forced his mind back to the present. 'I guess he didn't,' he repeated harshly. 'He never made it at all.'